LOVE AND ONLY WATER

Eva Asprakis

ISBN-13: 978-1-3999-3529-6

Cover design by: Mecob
Cover images: ©Shutterstock.com
Library of Congress Control Number: 2018675309
Printed in the United States of America

When you walk the streets of Nicosia, my father used to say, you walk on the wounds of history. The city aches, you can feel it. Walk quietly, walk carefully, walk gently. Can you hear the groans? Can you feel the pulse? And we walked and walked the narrow streets, down the alleys, round corners, and when we reached the Venetian Walls, he would put my small hand on the rough stone, cover it with his, and say 'Shh! Listen to the story on the other side.'

Nora Nadjarian, 'No-Man's Land'. This short story can be found in the anthology *Ledra Street*, published by Armida Books in 2006.

The South

One

Let me tell you about where I live. It is a city divided by time, one end tall and silver and slick, all glass. The other is made up of golden, often crumbling brick, low to dirt roads without any pavements. No glass in these windows. Boards cover a lot of them.

At this older end of the city, there is a wall.

Its brick is not like that of the surrounding houses. In fact, it mostly isn't made up of brick at all, but a miscellaneous tangle of barbed wire and barrels, whatever rubble our scrambling soldiers had to hand at the time of the conflict, when it was built. Hastily, in trembling fear. Loathing. Years have passed, the dust of several thousand hot days has plumed at the feet of running children, shabby cars spewing exhaust, bridal trains sweeping the steps of various Christian churches while Islamic calls to prayer have whined out overhead, most of these from the Other Side. The people are used to hearing them, here. Very few of them look up, let alone grit their teeth.

And yet they remember.

Those who weren't babes in arms or yet to be born, that is, those who had families and friends and homes that were lost. They were stolen, my grandfather insists in his affected English, hissing cigarette smoke, to this day. Andreas is his name. He comes from a place beyond the wall, beyond the other half of this severed city where the mountains meet the sea; he met the two of them like old friends every day as a young boy. Then came the invasion. He and his parents escaped to Prague—they were lucky enough to have a connection, the result of some distant marriage and tenuous though it was—where he finished his degree before they returned to this island, this city. Not their part of it anymore, not ever again. If their house was still standing it would long since have been occupied by strangers whose food tasted unfamiliar, whose language sounded harsher, who had no claim to the property, the photographs left in a swinging hurry on the walls inside, and who didn't care. There was no way of going back. My great grandparents had to build a new life, just blocks away from where they'd had one before, over the course of their mid-to-late years.

Now my grandfather is in his seventies, and he still dresses cartoonishly like a young Czech boy. Grey shorts to his knees, white socks hitched up out of penny loafers so they almost meet the hems, a collared shirt tucked into his belt, beneath braces and an ear-to-ear grin. When he is not talking about the conflict, he is boyish in character, too. He drinks with the novel gusto of one who has just turned the legal age, making plentiful toasts and jokes, and indulges in as many sweet treats as someone even younger might. When I was a child visiting in summertime, he would put together riddle after riddle out of disjointed words,

4

some in my first language, some in his; he would cock his head and sing 'come on' until I gave up and he told me the answer. It was silly, invariably.

"There once were two twins. One was twenty, the other was twenty-two. How can this be?"

I would shake my head.

"Twenty *too*. Not twenty-two." Such is his sense of humour.

His wife, Eliza, is not so easily entertained. Looking with beady eyes out of her wiry, overgrown bob, she startles and frets, warns of far-flung dangers that will likely never unfold and scrabbles to keep her loved ones close, ever desperate to protect them.

"Be careful," she said to me once, indicating the open window of her father's kitchen.

We were all there, sprawled in his first-floor flat beneath the whirring dark-wood fan. Everything else was—it still is—the terracotta and beige shades of the early sixties when it was built. There was the concentrated smell of coffee like toasted sugar paper, the darting of tongues and stifling heat. Pine trees outside, water tanks on flat-roofed buildings and dusty mountains beyond them. A clear sky.

"Daniela," my grandmother prodded me, "you must be careful not to fall."

I nodded, mumbled my thanks. My chair was metres away from the window and I had no intention of getting up from it. Or, after this exchange, of meeting my mother's eye. My

5

grandmother was attention-seeking, Deborah would doubtless complain to me later, there was no need for all her fussing. Wasn't it just ridiculous?

They are opposites, these women. Over the years, I have tried not to get caught in between the anticipatory worrying and 'what will be will be' mentalities that separate them. I try to remember—and to remind my father, when I see him struggling between mother and wife—that their differences are no one's fault. My mother comes from America, the land of the free and reactionary. When angered, she is aggressive; when upset, she is in tears; when happy, she becomes giddy; when hurt, she is downright frightening. My grandmother, meanwhile, has grown up here, in this city of uncertainty. In the simmering decade after the British withdrew their troops and our building was constructed, *her* mother, Katerina, was one of a thousand people to disappear. Nationalistic forces fanned the flames of derision between the island's two communities, which were not separated then. Men, women and children were dragged from buses and shops and murdered for their heritage. They were cast alone off riverbanks or into mass graves outside rural villages, never to be identified or even discovered. Inevitably there was the coup—our doing—followed by the invasion—*theirs*. Maddened by grief, Eliza's father took her to a village high in the mountains where she spent a formative two years taking cold tin baths outside, milking goats and growing vegetables, walking

6

miles to the nearest shop. It is strange to think now that someone who eats dinner out at a restaurant most nights used to get her water from a well, *if* it had rained enough. Perhaps it is not so strange that she looks for these issues before they present themselves. She feels safest feeling unsafe. This way, she can never be caught out.

My great grandfather is not wholly happy to have me here. I could make more of myself, he thinks, back in London where I was raised, surrounded by opportunities the likes of which are hard to come by in this other city. Older, dustier, on the verge of danger. At twenty-one, I am comparatively bright and boundless, I know. Everyone keeps saying it. But I don't feel that way, so I am here. You can't tell people that when they ask, of course. You can tell them you're undecided career-wise, that you're taking a year out to think some things through. You didn't go off travelling after school, so why not post university? Your friends all had gap years. Okay, so they actually went to university and you didn't, that's true, but it's not as though you've been doing nothing for the last three years, is it? You've been working, saving, wiling away time in a country that is not entirely your own while becoming more aware of it with every day that you are dark-haired, bold-browed, big-nosed and copper-skinned. You are other. People say 'oh' when they meet your parents—your thick-bearded, thick-accented father, particularly—and you have no

7

extended family to speak of, not locally. Not nationally. You don't even have a partner to confide in, anymore.

At this moment, I am in the square that joins the old part of the city with the new. It is early June, hotter than the hottest day in England but drier, so if I tell myself I am not too overwhelmed I might just believe it. It is easier to do this with the thin heat we get here than with humidity, my father, Jason, has told me. I don't know whether he is right. I have been here for all of two days. I have no job yet, no income, but I walk towards the glass front of a clothing shop anyway and feel the rush of air conditioning. My shoulders sag with relief. The sales assistant's do the same when she asks if I am Russian and I say no, though more out of disappointment. This happens often, I assume because of my blue eyes, the one feature my mother gave me. They are luminescent against my tanned skin, impossible to miss, something I was grateful for amongst my blonde classmates at school but which bothers me here. Because I am native, because I am not. To a worn sigh from its keeper, I leave the shop without making a purchase and continue across the square.

Golden brick crumbles before me, backed by barbed wire. I am staring at the makeshift wall that divides this city and sensing a similar structure inside myself, a buffer zone I can only cross from one side to the other and back again. I can never tear it down, can never unite my fractured selves. I don't know who I am, where I belong or even what I want. Perhaps here I can figure it out, reconcile myself as this country has strived to do for decades.

Two

On my third morning in the city, I lock up and descend the stairs to my great aunt Rita's. Her flat takes up the entire ground floor of the building in which I am staying. Her brother, my great grandfather, George, owns it. Over the years, his tenants have left and he has ceased to replace them. Instead he has moved in one family member after another as they have flown abroad to study or work, completed their course or quit their job and returned to this city unsure of their prospects, but with somewhere to live, thanks to him.

We almost did this once, my parents and I, when I was ten. My father had just left his office in Victoria and was walking towards the train station when a man he had noticed walking the other way, carrying a guitar by its strap over one shoulder, doubled back and clubbed him over the head with it, spitting and screaming something about him being a terrorist before some passers-by could restrain him. The police were called to the scene and within minutes, the man was arrested. Still, it was enough that we didn't feel safe in London for some time. The Arab world got terrible press and my father's appearance made him a target, his mother fretted over the phone, in tears. She begged him to shave his beard. I, too, grew terrified. Well into my teenage years, I remained convinced that if ever anyone seemed to want to harm me—a snarling older man, a hooded boy or a whole gang of them approaching—then it must be because of my perceived heritage. And so I forced myself never to let my gaze fall in fear, but to look these people straight in the eyes so they could see mine: western blue. Don't hurt me, I urged them silently, with my confidence-disguised cowardice, please.

Thankfully, my father was never attacked again. He went on with his commute from London's outskirts to its epicentre unaffected, it would seem, though he felt breathless with fear. I know he did. All the tension he held inside on those dreary mornings and dark evenings, he unleashed with his arms from his raincoat when he got home, and shook off the drops.

"The superiority complex in this country," he would slam the door saying. Or "The foreign policy", or "*The Daily Mail* . . ."

"*Alright*," my mother would respond, as though his incited rants were an attack on her. When a light bulb needed changing, she was quick to praise Jason for the fact that he was more his grandfather's son than his father's. Practical, self-sufficient. But when it came to his political tirades, she would curse this and bellow right back at him, her Boston accent all the brasher in anger.

Eventually, Jason stopped talking about moving us back home with him. Good, my great grandfather said, there were no jobs here for him anyway, certainly none that would ever match his English salary.

I can hear his voice as I round the building, push Rita's gate free of the vibrant pink bougainvillaea overgrowing it and step up onto her veranda. I can hear Andreas's voice, too. I imagine he is professing something equally political. He tends to be when talking to his father-in-law, like Eliza's new boyfriend, still, eager to engage and impress when really he enjoys less consequential talk. If George is to meet my grandparents for coffee, it is here, a floor below his own flat. They are all retired, and so they have lots of time for us, the uncertain. The stationary. Rita hasn't walked for fifteen years. I remember her watching the news a lot in my youth, arguing politics back at my other relatives. Now she hardly speaks at all, and the television is loud enough for me to hear it three floors up if I have a window open, otherwise it is off.

"Hallo, my love," Eliza greets me, always with a warm embrace. "Come in."

The front door remains open, but it is dark inside. You would never know, if you weren't told, about the floor-to-ceiling glass sliders that span the length of the veranda to either side. Rita keeps her shutters down day and night.

"Did you sleep well?"

"Yes, thank you. The flat is perfect," I say.

Behind a smile, I grit my teeth. Eliza must have noticed me repeating this phrase, surely. I don't know what else to do. I am staying in a family-owned property and have had the bills moved into my name for proof of address, but no one has mentioned a tenancy agreement or even a cash rate for rent. I feel overindulged. Worse than that, I feel insecure without a renter's rights, which makes me feel selfish, which must make me greedier and even more spoiled, thinking of myself and my needs before others' again. My family here would never turn me out or watch me go hungry, I know, and there are always my parents back in England, the box room that was mine for twenty-one years with the walls that were pink, then green and now a dusky grey; I can picture them. But it is still worth having a conversation, isn't it? To find out where I stand. Everyone has been so generous that the thought makes my skin shrink inwards. I don't know how to bring this up.

"Please. Make yourself comfortable," my grandmother says, indicating a space on the deep beige sofa that is penned in by wooden trolleys, sideboards, a coffee table. Lace webs every surface, as though spiders have spun their way through the darkness, inch by inch.

In the entrance hall, in the wide, high-ceilinged corridor and in several rooms beyond, bookshelves line the walls. They are stacked with French poetry, Rita's old medical journals and the tomes of geopolitical history that were her late husband's. There is the ancient smell of their pages and of wood varnish, and coolness emanating from countless china trinket dishes. Not one of them stands out from the rest.

13

"Thank you," I say, following my grandmother to the living room. The air inside feels closer.

"Daniela," Andreas smiles.

George does, too, though he does not look quite so relieved to be freed from their debate.

"How are you today?"

I am opening my mouth to answer that I'm well, it's good to see them both, when Rita coughs a full, hacking cough. I stop still. The sight of her slumped in her armchair is startling. In the months since my parents and I visited last summer, she appears to have deteriorated more than ever. What remains of her hair has shocked outwards, the mealy orange colour of a crayon that has been ground down to its last. Her eyes are a pearly brown, fixed upon me with wonder, no sign of recognition, and her ankles are swollen up to her knees. Poised beside her is a wheelchair. This is new. Her mouth hanging open, empty of words; everything vacant, her body of life. I think this seems worse because she was once *so* alive. I don't remember much of her with her husband, Elias, her with vigour or drive in her job as a paediatrician, but everyone says she was. Life and soul. Now she is body alone. She has chosen to be. It is very sad, my relatives say, and they fall quiet for a moment before continuing to talk amongst themselves as if she is not there at all. This, they maintain, is the most we can do for her now.

I hold my elbows in opposite hands.

"Daniela, please. There is something I must ask you." Andreas leans towards me. "How many months of the year have twenty-eight days?"

"Oh." Forcing my eyes to stay on him, not to stray back to my great aunt, I guess, "One of them? February."

"Just February? No. All months have twenty-eight days, at *least*."

"Of course . . ."

He falls back laughing and slapping his knees, looking first to his father-in-law for approval and then to his wife. One nods, the other rolls her eyes. I chuckle along until his hysterics die down into silence.

I clear my throat. "And how is Maria? I still haven't seen her."

At this, there is a murmur. My aunt Maria has lived on the top floor of the building since returning from London, where she did her art degree, ten years ago. I missed her sorely when she left, and have been keen to see her since my arrival.

"Maria went away with her friends for some days."

"I thought she was coming back last night."

"She was," my grandmother confirms. "She did. But they needed her to work today. She has a very busy schedule." She laughs, but it seems strained.

I notice that Andreas has turned away, even continued his talk of politics with George in a snappier, more aggravated tone than before.

15

"I see," I say, slowly.

Eliza pats my shoulder, softening once more as our conversation comes to a close. "Don't worry, my love. We will see her tomorrow."

Before a second silence can set in, George chirrups and I look up. In the doorway, upholding a broad wooden tray and a beaming smile I would know anywhere, is—

"Shehani!" I cry.

My grandparents are chuckling, saying the more casual hallos of people who are here all the time as I clamber over their legs and around the coffee table.

"Daniela, be careful," Eliza calls after me.

But when I stumble it is into Shehani's arms, strong from her persistent scrubbing and stirring. The smell of coffee rises from the tray she has put down, homely. All my life she has made it homely here, since the home*owner* has been unable to. That is what my grandmother hired her for, I suppose, but it hardly feels like she was hired at all, day to day. It feels like she is one of us, and I am as glad to see her as if she is.

When we draw apart, she takes my face in her hands and searches it. As if every inch of my skin, every stray lash and pockmark, is fresh water and her parched eyes are drinking it in.

"Beautiful, and so tall now . . ."

Self-consciousness tugs at me, but I don't pull away. I know I can't, that she needs me not to. Back in Sri Lanka, Shehani has a

16

daughter not many years younger than I am, though you would never believe it to look at her. She doesn't appear much older herself, possibly because of her skin tone. It is different to mine, to my family's, more like ground carob than ginger, hiding her age. Even this close to her, I can't see any sun damage or wrinkles, just her dark eyes shining, that radiant smile still on her face. It is unthinkable. That this woman, who has the most perfect white teeth I have ever seen, went abroad for work over a decade ago and hasn't laid eyes on her child since.

When she has wiped her tears, Shehani goes back into the kitchen and re-emerges with a traditional Sri Lankan sponge cake, soft with margarine and the toasted sweetness of vanilla, and takes a seat beside Rita. Ornate dessert plates are passed around. We scrape and batter them with our silver forks while Shehani feeds Rita, carefully, from a plastic spoon.

Then a cloud passes over the sun. Or so it seems, so soundless and cooling is the entrance of another person into the room. A woman so small she could fold herself into any corner, and so she does without a word. She is severe-looking, unsmiling. For a moment I think she has walked in off the street—the door is open, as always—but no one else seems concerned.

"Daniela, this is Atay," my grandmother tells me. As Rita's condition worsened, they needed more help with her. "Now Atay and Shehani will both live here, probably, until she goes into a hospice."

"Oh. I didn't realise . . ." Incompetent, I trail off, hold a forkful of sponge in my mouth until it turns to mush.

"Yes." Eliza's fringe crowds her furrowed brow. "We don't know when or if we will need to keep someone afterwards, for my father."

George gives a theatrical scoff and I laugh, gratefully.

"We will see."

"We will do our best," Shehani says, ever encouraging.

Glancing back at Atay—who has come from the Philippines, I am told—I shiver, though I cannot say why. I start fanning myself to appear as overwhelmed with the heat as everyone else. Rita has never had air conditioners installed, and relies solely on a cluster of plug-in fans for relief.

"Hi," I mumble.

Atay nods and says nothing. Again, I am compelled to look quickly away from her. Away from my great aunt, indisposed, away from my grandparents who are at once unsuspecting and suspect, I am sure of it, concealing something about Maria. My blushes fall at last upon Shehani, whose glowing smile, I notice, has disappeared without a trace.

Three

Despite the fact that they are almost strangers, Shehani is certain her daughter will go to university. She has always been certain. Before the girl was old enough to display talent or interest in anything that should have encouraged this, surely, Shehani was on a flight out of Sri Lanka, bound for the home country of her new employer: my grandmother. She has continued sending her wages back ever since, which must be meagre here, but which she says have funded the construction of a grand house there for her daughter, her aunt and her ailing mother. To this day, Shehani has not seen it. She is still saving up for her daughter's tuition, and won't divert any money towards a flight back in the meantime.

"Good morning," she calls, as I walk out of our building and across the street.

The sun is strong though it's early morning, glancing off the iron gate to Rita's veranda where Shehani is tending to the bougainvillaea. I smile over my shoulder but don't slow my pace, don't get drawn in. She is smothering me again with her eyes alone. I can feel them on my back, tugging at my throat like a child might my sleeve, making me feel guilty. For what? As much as I care for her, there is a part of me that resents this, a selfish part that could lash out, if I let it, at the suggestion of responsibility. It wasn't my choice to be born in London, to parents who weren't torn between leaving and letting me starve. They are not well off but they have done well enough, my mother a history teacher, my father in the civil service. It wasn't my fault that even in London, surrounded by opportunities, I didn't know what to do with my life, where to point so as to move in the right direction from start to finish. Perhaps there were *too many* options, I said to my mother before I left. How was I supposed to pick just one?

"You're not supposed to limit yourself to *none*, Daniela. I'll tell you that much."

Actually, she has told me plenty. About how I am making a mistake, I should have gone to university like her friends' children, I can't keep floating around without an aim anymore. For all the things she says I am doing wrong, however, she has yet to offer any insight into what I should be doing instead, what would be *right*. This is a person I have lived with for twenty-one years. She knows me well, far better than I like to admit, generally. By comparison, Shehani can't know her daughter at all, and yet she is adamant about what the girl—who must be almost eighteen by now—needs, what she wants and will do. Is this why I feel guilty? Because I have blatantly squandered the kinds of chances she broke up her family for? It's not as though we could have swapped places, the strange, defensive part of me thinks. But I suppose that doesn't matter.

In twenty minutes, I am downtown. The square where modern meets timeworn is littered with teenagers, some loud and in motion, with money—it is evident in the shopping bags swinging from their fingertips, their carefree smiles and keeling laughter—while others are less fortunate. Their eyes are darting and soulful, their clothes too long and thick for the summer, while I am sweating through my T-shirt. These boys have come from across the sea, I assume, where differences are not so clearly marked as with piled bricks or barbed wire. Not stoppered by them either. Their skin is a shade darker than mine, and those who don't scuff their trainers as I pass by their pigeon-plagued benches call after me in a language I don't understand.

Without looking back, I pick up my pace, hear my breaths coming ragged and then a chime, the blast of air conditioning as I enter a shop. Stop, blink.

"Hallo," an immaculately bronzed girl greets me.

I blink again, take in her long lashes and manage a smile, at last.

She returns it. Then, in English, "Are you Russian?" she asks.

The boys don't see me leave the shop in another sigh of cool air. Deeper into the old city, on a pedestrianised street beneath white and yellow sails strung together for shade, is a coffee shop. It stands out from the many others for its jungle of hanging plants, dim lamps and mismatching chairs and tables; I can make them out through the glass front once my eyes are accustomed.

'Chest' is written in bold red above the shutters pushed to one side. A strange name for a coffee shop, but there is something about it that resonates with me. I fall back a step, remembering; this is one of a few places that my grandmother has told me is hiring. She knows people, she has said, she could talk to them and sort something out for me this week. She is desperate for me to agree, I can tell, to get a job somewhere she knows, desperate to know when and by what route I will go in for each shift, and, most vitally, what time to expect me home. She wants to know that she *can* expect me home, as she could not her mother. But I want to have a look around before I commit to anything, consider the kind of work I might do here. Evading the gaze of a waitress, I continue down the street.

My first paid job was at a café. Before that, as part of my Duke of Edinburgh's Award, I volunteered at a local church running the children's group on a Saturday. I have never been sure about God, though, any god. It wasn't long before my supervisor questioned my questioning, my furrowed brows and cocked head. Was this really a good fit? For me, he went on. Was there much in it? I looked around the cavernous space and replied, apologetically, that that's what I had been wondering.

The rest of my volunteering I did at an Oxfam shop where Travis's *The Invisible Band* was the only CD I could stomach from three shelves of donations. Christmas compilations, *Now That's What I Call* albums. Before a customer could buy it, I did. I stashed it under the till and played it on a loop all the time I was there. Three months, that was supposed to be—less with the few weeks I had done at the church already—but I ended up staying for over a year. Outside school, I wasn't so devoted to any hobbies or friends that I couldn't spare one day a week, and I enjoyed feeling like I was doing something good. Really good, for the world and not just for me. Then school ended. So did my first—and last—relationship. I suffered through sixth form with a broken heart, and found the goodwill and the selflessness to be in increasingly poor taste.

Finally, I defected to making money full time. The world took a hit while I served bubbling cappuccinos, sweet with syrup or thin with plant milk, and refused customers 'large flat whites'; those just became lattes, my manager fumed. Never mind the injustice of poverty.

Several doors down is a second-hand clothes shop, also in need of staff. I stop outside to adjust my waistband, let my eyes narrow from the slanting-lettered sign in the window to the darkness beyond. Sweat on my midriff. Sweat on my thumbs and, now that I think about it, between every strand of my hair and my toes. Rather than a rush of coolness there is a musty smell when I step inside, which doesn't match the bright chime that sounds overhead. This isn't a charity shop, as such. Those don't exist here, not like in England. Anything you don't want, you either give to a church—if you can find one that will accept it—or throw into a charity 'bin', even if it is still perfectly useful. Shops like this one will take select garments off your hands, but they'll pay you nothing in return, nor give any proceeds from the onward sales they make to charity. I do find this strange. If your castoffs aren't going to a good cause, what's the point? There is more incentive for people to sell things online.

Still, there are several women pushing through the dense racks of clothes, all with lines of muted panic or deep focus etched into their faces. They are not like the girls in the glass-fronted shop I burst into, who pawed at brand new things looking bored, aloof or disinterested, more heavily made-up and sweeter smelling.

"Daniela?"

I turn around. It isn't until a familiar face breaks out into a smile that I realise I am frowning, and soften my expression in return.

"Maria," I start, forgetting the moth-eaten quiet of our surroundings.

The women whose nerves are similarly frayed at the edges watch us, wary, as we crash into each other's arms.

"What are you doing here?"

"I'm working," she says, as we draw apart.

"Here?"

She nods.

I'd had no idea. My smile fades at the corners as I remember her dream to be an artist, a painter. All my life she has wanted that, and most of hers. As a child, I sat for hours and watched her make deft strokes with pencils and brushes of various sizes, shapes getting more severe before she filled them with colour. The fan hummed overhead; the beads that hung from it clicked together every few rounds it made. I sat cross-legged on a beanbag or hung from the ladder up to my aunt's bed, letting the air hit my face rhythmically, begging her to teach me her talent. She was a teenager at the time, more like *my* sister than my father's since there were fourteen years between them and only ten between us. Never content with standing still or leaving space for inexpressiveness, she didn't constrain herself to an easel. The wall was her canvas, she told me, the room was. The world.

I search her face. Her heavy-lidded brown eyes, hooked nose and dark hair, long and matted from frequent trips to the sea so I can never tell if it is naturally wavy or just choked with salt, unbrushed. "Are you happy here?" I ask her.

She nods through a confessional shrug. "It is a lot of hours. We need more staff."

"But you got away this week?"

At this, she shakes her head. She has missed what I said, or missed my meaning. I repeat the question in her first language, my second.

25

"Ah," she says. Her eyes widen as she comprehends me and then, just as my grandmother did, she narrows them. Closes her mouth and all further questions down with a thin smile. "Yes. I went for a few days. But I'm back now."

Four

The next morning, a Sunday, my aunt is absent again. My grandparents and I have gathered at George's and there is an empty chair. It is one of eight with a wooden frame and a turmeric-orange velvet covering, too hot to sit back in.

"I thought she was working later today," I say, frowning.

No one says anything back. The fan is whirring, the radio on, the woodcocks calling beyond the window. And yet the silence is tangible.

My great grandfather is making coffee over what looks like a Bunsen burner and reminds me of chemistry, just as the experiments I did in class, heating metals and acids, used to remind me of this. This tradition, my culture. Meanwhile, my grandfather watches as if it is a barbeque. Men move towards open flames everywhere to feel the heat on their faces as they size each other up. These two have been at it for years, and still Andreas critiques George's method; how high with water he fills his pot, how long he holds it over the flame and how much sugar he adds to it.

"She is out at the moment. We will see her later," my grandmother intones, beside me.

The kitchen is starting to simmer with a smell like toasted sugar paper. Andreas is muttering his disapproval over George's shoulder, George shaking his head in quiet defiance, draining the pot into two short cups and holding one out on its saucer for us to see. It is full to the brim.

"Well, okay." With a shrug, Andreas takes it. "Bravo. Thank you."

George nods and they both chuckle.

"Daniela, do you want one?"

"Or a Nescafe? It is very strong, that one," my grandmother cautions me.

To be polite, I heed her warning. My grandfather spoons the weaker powder into a mug for me, equips her with a glass and a bottle of water from the fridge and takes a seat. No caffeine for Eliza; it is dangerous, she says. As always, George places himself at the head of the table, bringing with him a tray of fresh pastries. We tuck in.

"So," Eliza says, through a lip-smacking mouthful of filo and goats' cheese, "have you thought any more about what you would like to do for a job?"

Pastry flakes off a sausage roll as I move it to my plate. I think of the second-hand clothes shop, how my aunt—who was set on her dream of becoming an artist—grew accustomed to its darkness, unable to see her way back out.

"Not retail," I decide aloud.

"Not retail. Okay," Eliza chortles, with her usual nervous energy. She dusts her fingers free of flakes over her plate. "Well, there are some other options. Do you have something particular in mind?"

"Erm." I look down at my portion, still untouched.

As a matter of fact, I do.

Curious, I walk into town wearing black denim shorts and an oversized T-shirt. This is instantly regrettable in the extreme heat, but I am from this island. I know that colour marks the tourists. Residents are clad in this heat-absorbent shade year round, as if in defiance or show of the fact that they—we—can take it. We barely notice it, in fact. The few patterns I do see are still backed by black. A white shirt or blouse is acceptable, beneath a black blazer, if you work in an office. Less so if you are in a different field. Retail, for example.

The 'staff wanted' sign is still up in the window of the shop where my aunt works. Through it, I can see that another woman is behind the till. I wait a few moments and, when Maria still doesn't appear, I take a turn of the room to see if I can glimpse her in the back, sorting through stock or paperwork. Neither. The door hits my heels with its luminous chime as I stop dead outside. My grandparents were misled, or mis*leading*: she is nowhere to be seen.

Pushed onwards by the sun on my back, I drift deeper into the old city. I barely notice where I am going. I am still reeling from where I have been, where my aunt should have been and wasn't. A part of me dares to hope that she is hidden away with a palette and brushes, skipping work, unbeknownst to her parents, to pursue her dream of becoming an artist. This part of me is foolish, I know. But a dream should translate into reality, shouldn't it? Ambition into direction. That kind of vision for the future is something I lack, and have always envied people like her. I can't explain why. I feel sure, though, that Maria is not lying to my grandparents, that they know where she is and are lying to me. Andreas and Eliza, the kindest, most accepting people in the world, ever open-armed. Dread gnaws at my insides. What could their daughter possibly be involved in that they, of all people, cannot forgive her for it?

At the end of a dusty street beneath shuttered buildings and a wide white umbrella, I am stopped. Several people stand before me, ten or fifteen of them perhaps, shifting from side to side on their sandaled feet. Every one of them is dressed in colour. As I take a step sideways to peer around them, it occurs to me what they are queueing for. Indeed, there are the cones and blue UN tapes marking the crossing point past security. Armed soldiers stationed here and, just metres beyond them, more waiting on the Other Side. I fall back a step. Our boys look young, no older than me, with guns like biceps, bulging, too big for their slender arms. The desert heat of July and August is yet to come, and it is too hot already for the full camo they are wearing. Looking at them, I can understand why two years' military service is mandatory for boys when they turn eighteen. Who else would choose this? Beads of sweat on their temples, visibly trickling; sightseers agog, treading the dirt of the Other Side back into ours with them. And there, beyond the divide, guns in the hands of men whose grandfathers slaughtered ours for this land, ready to be fired.

I don't like being this close to the wall. It has always unnerved me. It feels like prodding at a scabbed wound, and makes me want to withdraw quickly, before any fresh blood can spill out.

"Excuse me," someone says, in English.

I wheel around and see a balding man, herding his heavyset wife and two daughters. The girls are young, their light eyes wide and fixed on the weapons over my shoulder.

"Are you waiting?" their father asks me, with a florid motion.

Although I don't need to—I can understand him perfectly—I turn to look where he is pointing. From the line of people shuffling forwards in front of me, to the stern-faced UN officers in their booth like a shipping container, to the border. And beyond. A breeze drags at the dust around my heels. It blows past them all and settles at the shadowy feet of someone on the Other Side. Except she is not there, not really; she is a stubborn memory, forcing her way back into my mind's eyeline. Her name springs to the tip of my tongue and I bite down on it like too harsh a truth, or a fear that I am wary of speaking into being.

"I . . ." Don't know. I shake my head. Why don't I know? Saying no should be easy. To cross over would be an insult, an outrage, to every member of my family. I have never done it before and I have no intention of doing it now. Do I? "Erm . . ."

It is at this moment that I see her, glaring at me from down a narrow side street, in shadow. A short, sharp-eyed woman; tangible, unlike the girl from my past. I forget the sun on my back. For as long as I can remember, Sundays have been Shehani's day off, and yet here is her new colleague, out of the house, alone. Instinct sends me back a step before her name comes to mind. Then it does, *Atay*, and I fall out of line completely.

"No," I stammer, "I'm not waiting. Go ahead."

"Thanks," says the Englishman, not without a puzzled frown.

He has stepped in between his family and I, as if I might pose a threat to them, but I am too shaken to care. I have been caught out, I feel, inexplicably. By stumbling upon the border and not turning away at once, I have done something terribly wrong. My only hope is that Atay, my witness, will keep her solemn silence.

Five

I am on my way inside when I see George, crouching in the dirt amongst stray cats. A few of them are familiar, one grey with a white underbelly, another with a fold in its ear. I walk past the evidence of his feeding them each day, puddles of water and scraps of meat leftover from our family lunches. Sometimes bread, like my mother and I used to throw to the ducks in Wells Park when no one was watching. She grumbles that he'll attract rats doing that, since the cats don't eat it. But his affection for them makes me smile.

Looking up, he returns my grin and I cannot believe he is ninety, that he grew up in the mountains, walking miles and riding donkeys in a time before cars. He remembers shillings and the conflict, and a conflict before that one. His parents' house had two bedrooms, one that he shared with them and his four siblings; the other housed the goats they kept to milk and breed and sell. He is ninety and can still fold himself down to his knees, his joints are so supple. His organs, too. Every part of him remains healthy.

This is because he follows 'the old diet', he has told me. The food we eat now, the food we are known for on this island, worldwide, is actually very new to us. The skewered meat and cheese that we market as traditional used to be eaten once a week, as a luxury, at most.

"And the rest of the days, it was beans!"

My great grandfather takes pride in this revelation. He still prepares his beans, diligently, a day in advance, squeezing lemon juice over some varieties and dousing others in grape vinegar. All of them he slathers in olive oil.

This, his descendants agree, over our grilled cheese and kebabs, must be the secret to his immortality.

"Hallo," George waves at me, from the ground.

"Hi," I say.

I hope he keeps up his olive oil consumption. I want to hear him chuckle like this for years to come, but I cannot look directly at him as he does. Not today, after what I came close to doing. Where I came close to going, for reasons I cannot explain.

With an almost imperceptible effort, my great grandfather gets to his feet. "I was just checking the temperature," he tells me, dusting his palms off on his trousers. His moustache moves as he talks, giving the impression of a hand puppet. It is thick white against his ripe brown skin, overhanging his top lip as his nose overhangs it, having grown bigger and more hooked as he has aged.

"How hot is it today?"

"It is hot, yes."

I keep my gaze fixed on his lower face as he talks, still too guilty to meet his eyes. I can picture them, wide and wise with all they have seen, enough to make him this quiet conspirator; he tracks the heat with thermometers on the walls of his flat and here, in the shade outside the building, and insists that the met office is not to be trusted. They lie to us, he says. All through summer, they claim it is cooler than it actually is so that the government won't have to send workers home. George is always keeping an eye on this, on *them*. It is another thing that we as a family chortle at, shaking our heads as if it is quaint, charming and ultimately quite silly. But his suspicions are founded.

On the night of the invasion, George took almost twenty people into this building, relatives and neighbours who feared their own homes were too central, or else not strong enough to withstand the impending siege. They slept shoulder to shoulder on the floor of Rita's flat, and when George tried to retrieve something from upstairs—a grainy photograph of his parents, I believe, the only one in existence—they did not let him; it was safer on the ground.

News spread of the aggressors' advances, close to the city. Too close for comfort, George decided, and he fled to his childhood village the next morning with Rita, Elias and Eliza. My grandmother. She was nineteen at the time, but recalls that journey with the blatancy of a first memory. The beginning of something, the beginning of life or her understanding of it as wild with terrors. Because she had been under ten at the time of her mother's disappearance, no one had told her the full story. George would tell it now, he said, his eyes like the muzzles of two smoking guns in the rear-view mirror. Eliza shrank into her seat, her lungs shuddering with anticipation. But she did not get the full story, not the one she had wanted with a coherent beginning, middle and end. No one knew it. Anxiety set its cold grip upon her heart.

The road through the mountains was frenzied with carloads of people doing the same thing they were. George, Eliza, Elias and Rita spent four nights in his childhood home. The house was made of stone up to their knees, then mud and dung, donkey hair and straw, not poured concrete like their newly built home in the city. Gunshots echoed over peaks and valleys. There was no telling how far off they were.

In the darkness, Rita squeezed her brother's hand. "It's just like it used to be," she whispered, while her husband slept on the other side of her.

But their parents were gone, their siblings elsewhere—at least one of them was in the thick of the fighting—and the goats no longer chewed their way, noisily, through the neighbouring room. They no longer came inside at all. That had changed in their lifetimes, just as everything else was changing. Rita would adapt well, George thought. She had Elias. She was bolder in the face of things then. Long after she drifted off, he was kept awake by the warmth of his daughter beside him; he tossed and turned over in his mind the fact that he must keep her safe, somehow, with none of Katerina's maternal instincts to help him.

When a broadcast aired on the radio, informing them that it was safe to return to the city, everyone wanted to go except George. He remained wary, but eventually agreed to accompany his family. They had driven less than halfway there when another broadcast urged them to turn back; things were unstable in the capital. Urbanite Elias, having grown restless with the bugs and the shrubs and the outdoor tin-bathing of the mountains, was determined that he and Rita would continue to the city regardless, to see what state their home was in. The family had pooled all their money to build it and were relieved to find it unoccupied, still theirs. This was more than could be said for others.

George drove his daughter back to the village, disillusioned with the government's ability to protect them, and so they stayed put for the next two years. Things were still unstable in the capital, he maintained, long after the fighting had stopped. They always would be. But Eliza had no prospects when she came of age, hidden away from jobs and men. She needed to be in the city, Rita said, then shouted and wailed until George gave in and they moved back to their flat. At a protest in the centre Eliza met Andreas, whose silliness distracted her, for gorgeous moments, from her state of fret. She married him and fell pregnant with

Jason that same year, leaving George to his conspiracy theories and the occasional night spent in the mountains, alone.

I watch as he drives his thermometer further into the soil beneath his shoe, startling a kitten from the undergrowth.

"They should send us home soon," he says, referring once more to the government, to the rising heat, "but they won't."

"We *are* home," I smile, still not meeting his eye.

My great grandfather wags a finger and says, "Good thing. Otherwise . . ."

Bidding him goodbye, I climb the stairs to my flat, take a bottle of water from my fridge and stand at the kitchen counter, gulping some down. The cold burns my throat. I lower my glass, look out the window. I see the flag of the nation that invaded this one carved, gleeful, goading, into the mountainside above what is now their half of the city, according to them and to no one else. No international governing body has condoned their snatching of it away from us. To this day they remain an illegal state, and still the tourists flock to their beaches, ignorant or selfish. Irresponsible, I think, in any case. I am still staring at the flag when I remember how close I myself came to the crossing point, just this afternoon—I could have stayed until after dark to see them light it up in flashing neon, as they do every night—and I feel my mouth turn down in disgust. No love lost, I think. Except there was.

Six

Two days have passed since I encountered Atay at the border and I am back in the old part of the city, still jumpy, beneath the strung-up flags of yellow and white. People move slowly under their shade, stopping in at every third shop for the air conditioning, if nothing else. I know this pattern. I follow it, here.

In my anxiousness to get away from Atay, to get away from my family whom she might yet make suspicious of me, I have decided to escalate my job search. The first place I go into is the coffee shop my grandmother told me was hiring, Chest. The red lettering does not look as bright as it did with the afternoon sun on it, creating a glare on the surrounding glass, but it is still bold. Strongbox, I think. That is one meaning of the word 'chest'. A fortified container that precious things can be kept safe inside. I take off my sunglasses.

A waitress watches as I weave my way in through the mismatching tables and chairs. She does not smile, does not say a word when she brings me the menu, or when I give her my order.

"Thank you," I call after her.

Thank *you*, she would have replied, if she were a customer back at Oxfam and I were the one serving her. She would have left happy. Everyone did; I made sure of that. I sigh to think of trading that quietly fulfilling job in for yet another vapid one, of returning to debates of what is and is not decaf with pernickety customers in place of those who were happy to help, however little they had themselves. But it must be done. I am feeding myself now, even if not paying rent.

When my drink lands on the table, I look up to thank the stony-faced waitress a second time and catch my breath. Someone is watching me, startling me. *Atay*. No. She is at Rita's, I soothe myself. Only then am I able to look back at the boy across the room. It is the strangest thing. Again, I catch him watching me and feel as if I have burned my tongue, but when I retreat into my tall glass and tug at the straw, eyes down, I know this cannot be true. My coffee is cold and milky. His gaze is dark and fixed, still, upon me. I want to sink even deeper into my cushioned seat. With its rattan arms and back, it is one of two set at this low table in the corner. The other is glaringly empty.

I let my eyes flick upwards. Across the lamplit room—it is den-like, in spite of the morning sunshine—he is smiling. The long-haired boy with the high cheekbones and a cigarillo between his teeth. My breaths come shallowly. I lean into a longer one and hear my glass hit the table with a thud.

He has stopped looking at me.

Now his smile is turned upon someone else, a slender girl sitting opposite him. Beside her is another boy, shorter-lashed and neater-haired. His brother? His friend? The boyfriend of this girl, or is that my long-haired boy? There is a sensation like something unfurling in my stomach, releasing a sour fluid. Bitter disappointment. Over what? This is unlike me, I scold myself, sucking back what remains of my coffee. Hollow air sounds through the straw. It is ludicrous of me to sit here fantasising about what might happen between us, as if I am regularly approached by strangers in coffee shops.

Stuffing a note into the shot glass with my bill, I sling my bag over my shoulder and tumble outside. The cobbles compel me further from the door.

"Hey," someone says, behind me.

A cheap chain clothing store, a low-ceilinged tourist trap. I continue weighing up the shops ahead until I feel a hand on my shoulder.

"Hey. Sorry," says the long-haired boy, when he sees my eyes widen.

He is even better looking in the sunlight, with a white scar under one brow that makes his left eye gleam green-brown. I notice for the first time how wicked his smile is before he bows to light his cigarillo.

"Did I scare you?"

"No."

"Are you sure?"

At my blush, his grin broadens.

"Maybe a little."

41

Another apology. This one, though, seems less sincere. "I'm glad I caught you. My friends couldn't believe I'd even try."

"Why not?" I ask, as in the sweltering heat I dare to wonder if he was as taken with me as I was with him, on sight. I wonder if I am someone who people might be taken with generally, here. My blonde friends back in England called me 'exotic' and 'curvy' in the same purring tones they used to cheer each other up. They envied me my tan, my thick hair. Nothing else. Not my widespread nose or my sturdy thighs, certainly. Am I envied for those things here?

"Because I'm too good for you."

I blink.

The long-haired boy shrugs and lets out a full chuckle as I falter at his insult. He is joking, he assures me. "I'm Paris. What's your name?"

"Daniela."

"Daniela," he repeats.

It sounds good coming with the smoke out of his crooked mouth, beneath his eyes that seem to dart and stay intent on mine all at once. I push my sunglasses up my nose and feel the slick of sweat on their frame.

"How old are you?"

"Twenty-one. How old are you?"

"About the same age," Paris says, "at heart."

I stifle a laugh, raise my eyebrows.

"Give me your number and I'll tell you."

At the shock of his boldness, my laughter escapes.

"Come on, it's a fair trade. I'll even throw in my surname."

The cigarillo has burned down to an ember between his fingers. People pass by us from the far end of the cobbled street. I imagine them thinking that we are already a couple, since we have been standing together for so long. Then I realise that I don't know how to say no to us becoming one, or flirt my way towards yes; I lack the experience.

And so I take out my phone, unceremoniously. Clutch it in both hands. "Should I get your number as well, or . . ?"

"You will," Paris says, sliding his away with ease.

I stare after it as though he has pocketed a piece of me with it.

"All in good time, Daniela. It was nice meeting you."

"You too," I murmur.

He stubs out his cigarillo and goes back into Chest.

Its last light singes the edge of my vision even as I watch it get stepped on, start greying. All the way home I cast around myself, thinking I have seen it again. But there is no smoke, no spark, no Paris. Not until late in the evening, when his first message lights up my bedroom.

'Twenty-seven', it says.

'Aren't you forgetting something?'

'What?'

'Your surname'.

'You'll have to get that out of me over a drink'.

My thumbs fall from my phone. Lying in bed on my back, I am overcome with remembering the last time someone made me feel this way. The only time, in all my life. It was years ago, and I haven't been sure enough of myself to let it happen again since. The light from my phone screen creates a ghostly sheen on the ceiling. Here is Paris now, out of nowhere, at another time in another place. Is it the right time and place? I don't know. But I can feel my heartbeat in my stomach as I haven't since I was fifteen, and the certainty of being sought after is enticing. It is a comfort, when you are unsure, to be with someone who knows what they want: you. I remember it lightening my frantic load. But was that enough then? Will it be now?

'What do you think?' His message glows.

I take a deep breath and type my reply.

Seven

Back in England, I went to school with a girl from this city. The Other Side of it, she admitted, a smile creeping across her chin. Her eyes were darker than mine, which I felt flash with jealousy, as if she had outdone me in this way. They were guarded, too, as she watched for my response. Beyza was her name. Having just started secondary school, we were desperate to stand out and fit in, two things which were total opposites and yet one seemed to equal the other. Like our paler peers, we cared more than anything about achieving them. More than we did about our disjointedly shared heritage, it appeared, as we made a show of squabbling over whose island this was before either one of us was old enough to understand the other's argument. I could barely comprehend my own, while onlookers laughed and understood even less. I shake my head to think of it now. The mockery we made of our families' suffering, the callous ignorance with which we carried it on.

We were split up into separate classes and drifted, then, for a couple of years. It seemed to me as if everyone else was getting to know who they were in this time, or where they were going at least, but by fifteen I still had no clue. My frantic nail-biting and window-gazing led me to move down a maths class, where I was sat next to Beyza again. She smiled at me, that same timid smile.

45

Her lips were fuller, I noticed, as were her breasts. She had grown into her body as I had mine; we shared the same overripe figures that were distinctive of our part of the world. It's funny, in the city where I am now, she is from The North and I am from The South, but in England we were simply from the east, both of us. Indistinguishable from one another once we let the wall crumble and slide, there was nothing between us.

There was something, however, between Beyza and Vicky. Something strong, she assured me, there had to be. We were hunched in a stony corner of the Rookery Gardens near where she lived at the time. It was March. Like our parents, we were always overdressed for England, always nestling into our necklines with our heads bowed, our eyes up. I was scowling and spluttering my way through a first cigarette. Beyza was lighting her second, reading out the texts she had exchanged with our classmate the previous night.

"Eleven p.m.," she said. "And the next one, two a.m." There sounded a smack as she let the back of her hand hit her thigh, then raised it for another drag, wide-eyed. "*Two a.m.*, Dani. What does that even mean?"

We sat discussing this matter, dissecting it message by message. Clearly Vicky was attracted to Beyza but in denial about her sexuality, or something else that left my friend as soothingly blameless. She was amazing, and Vicky would be lucky to have her.

In the following months, I helped Beyza draft more messages and a letter, once, in her looping handwriting. I had advised against the latter since she had professed her feelings already and been rejected. As I feared, the response came more harshly this time: *no*. Vicky was straight. Back in the Rookery Gardens, I held my friend while she cried and tried my luck, fists clenched and damp, in shop after tatty shop until I was served forty straights and a litre of Smirnoff at her behest. The air filtered from my lungs in shaky relief. Her head slumped back on my shoulder against the craggy wall of a flowerbed.

"Thank you," she croaked, I was a good friend. The best.

She said she would get me some weed to try as proper thanks from her on-off older boyfriend Pete, who smoked a lot. Because he was self-conscious about the size of his penis, he preferred head to full sex, which suited her just fine, apparently. She liked smoking with him; she didn't love sex with any man. Meanwhile, I was embarrassed by my lack of experience and keen to make up for it quickly. Perhaps agreeing to this would open up doors for me, I thought, even if only in my mind, make me see clearer who I was or would be. Perhaps it would simply make me a druggie, and even that would be better than stunted and uncertain as I was otherwise.

It was a grey day above the Rookery Gardens when Beyza rolled the joint, lit it. I was fascinated by the grinding twist of the plastic mechanism she put it through first, the sheer paper sheet that looked as though it would melt into her tongue like boiled sugar when she licked it. There was the catch of her lighter, bright against the rocks and the weather, and then a putrid smell. I tried not to wrinkle my nose or cough when the substance hit the back of my throat, though the air was getting rapidly thicker. I looked up. The first droplets of rain webbed my lashes. I blinked them clear and then the park was awash with rain coming down as hard as it had come on fast.

"Quick," Beyza squealed, hunching her shoulders and bowing her head as she sucked the joint down to its last, passed it back to me soggy and started to run.

Not knowing how to dispose of the thing, I clutched it between my fingers, extinguished and limp, until she noticed when we were waiting to cross a road outside the park and tossed it away from us. We ran back to her attic bedroom in her parents' house, which was so thin as to appear insecure, like it was sucking in. Everything shifted and creaked beneath our bare feet thumping up the stairs. We were like children again, chasing each other around in a fight over our island and laughing, panting, falling back onto her bed.

She slipped easily into talking about all the clichéd existential stuff once she had caught her breath, and I indulged her by listening although I remained too self-aware to say much myself about how big the world was, how small we all were. It embarrassed me. Over hours, the dozy warmth in my arms and feet faded. It was a spring evening both inside me and out; it had been pleasant all day, but the sun was not yet consistently hot enough for the earth to hold its heat overnight. And so I stood. We hugged goodbye. When we drew apart, her eyes were shining and her plump lips were stretched thin in a blushing smile. Then they were on mine and I was blinking, confused, pulling back, saying no. We shouldn't, I couldn't.

"Why not?" she asked.

Perhaps it was the way her voice cracked when she said it, but it occurred to me then that I didn't have an answer. Not a good one anyway, none I could use to say I was straight that would be categorically true. Beyza was not unattractive to me. Quite the opposite—I was actively drawn to her. Whether because she was familiar or forbidden, I wasn't sure. She was from my city and she was not, the only person I could talk to about it who would really understand, besides my father.

We kissed a lot after that, when we got high. We held hands when we walked down the street, which was most weekends until the end of year eleven, the end of our GCSEs, and most days the long summer afterwards.

"I love you," she said to me.

I loved her, too, but I still wasn't sure in what way. Our relationship could only get so serious; Beyza had had girlfriends before, I knew, but her parents did not. She hid me from her family as the women in it hid their hair from everyone but their husbands, god-fearing. They had no idea of the goings-on in her life, nor did I inform my parents of those in mine. Coming out seemed too decisive as it was, let alone coming out as the girlfriend of someone from the Other Side. And so I did not.

When September came, we started at different sixth forms. Our year group mixed with the local boys' school for these last two years and Beyza's parents, the little that they knew, didn't want her getting distracted. They sent her to an all-girls college while I stayed put and befriended, loosely, both the new boys and girls. Two or three weeks in, I made the mistake of mentioning some of their names to Beyza. I was lying on her bed at the time, breathing deeply, contentedly through my nose and feeling shivers of aftershock rush down from my hips. We were talking in murmurs. Then she was up on one elbow half-shouting, demanding to know who these people were and how I dared spend all my time with them when she was miserable without me. *Miserable*, she cried. I was stunned, then defensive. She was on her feet being unreasonable, telling me to get out, go and never come back. Afterwards I wished I had reassured her, but at the time all I could feel was revulsion, actual revulsion, as I stared with my lips curled at hers, still wet from between my legs. I hated that on the train home I could taste her, too, and I stormed straight upstairs to wash her away with all my tears.

We haven't spoken since.

Eight

I am panting when I open the door to Eliza, a balled up rag in my hand.

"Daniela," she smiles, then wrinkles her nose. "You are cleaning?"

"The ants are back."

At this, we share a grimace. I found three or four on the kitchen counter when I first arrived, and got rid of them only to find another two on the wall this morning. It is astonishing that they will climb so many storeys up to get in. I might be impressed by their determination, as sheer as the side of this building they have scaled, if I wasn't so disgusted by them. My compulsively clean mother never had ants in her kitchen, never had to follow Eliza's advice to keep it that way.

"Did you put vinegar on them?"

"Yes," I say, raising my pungent rag in demonstration. "I'm just doing it now. Shall I meet you downstairs?"

With my grandmother gone, I return to the poorly sealed fuse box around which I think the ants have been getting in. I soak the rag in yet more grape vinegar and run it in arcs over the wall. It leaves a sheen like sweat, and I in turn wipe my brow.

"That should keep them away. The smell," Eliza clarifies, when I have joined her at Rita's.

"Me too," I laugh.

I am grateful when everyone else joins in, Eliza, Andreas, George, Maria and Shehani. With my great aunt lolling back in her armchair, it is easy to be sombre, to think only of mortality. Shehani's smile fades.

"Good morning, Atay," my grandmother says.

Fear falls through my stomach at Atay's slinking entrance. She nods and says nothing. Nothing, I try to soothe myself, she doesn't even make eye contact. She will not say anything about where she saw me earlier this week. I am being paranoid. Although, I observe as Shehani stands up, clearly I am not projecting.

"I will make coffee," she declares, and leaves the room.

When she comes back, there is a nod or a whisper or something, there must be, because Eliza follows her once again over the threshold. A spoon rattles atop the tray she has left behind.

"What?" my grandmother frets. "What is it, Shehani?"

They disappear out onto the veranda and their voices die off.

The smell of coffee comes over me as if I have been submerged in it. Andreas leans in, passes one of the shorter cupfuls to George and takes the other for himself. There is the sound of him sipping like someone blowing up a balloon, filling the silence with colour, then a clatter as he returns his cup to its saucer. I pass Maria her Nescafe.

"Thank you," she says.

And the balloon is burst.

"Daniela, tell me. What is this?" My grandfather raises a finger and enunciates, clearly, "If I have it, I do not share it. If I share it, I do not have it."

"Hmm." Mug in hand, I sit back. A remembrance of the Sri Lankan sponge Shehani baked the last time we were here gives rise to goose bumps on my tongue. I try to focus on it, cake, how it cannot be both had and eaten. Can the word for 'had' also mean 'shared' in my second language? Atay darkens the corner of my vision so I cannot concentrate, cannot think through this last connection. "Is it cake?" I guess, regardless.

Andreas spreads his palms. "Cake? That would be much better."

He falls back cackling and I glimpse gaps in his teeth from too much sugar, too few trips to the dentist, driving his wife to dismay. Going to doctors of any kind is too grave for my grandfather; he is afraid to. Eliza goes constantly, fearing that the alternative could be *her* grave.

Falling quiet, he leans towards me. "The answer is, a secret."

"Ah," George says.

Maria giggles. "That's a good one."

53

I smile in agreement but can think of no response. Then Rita groans, a guttural noise that sends me curling from my seat.

"Excuse me," I say, and I start towards the bathroom.

I have to walk past the front door to get there, but I don't catch more than a murmur from outside. All my ears are concerned with, shrinking in to both sides of my head, is Rita's distress. My eyes, too, are watering. To see the bounties of her travels—a hanging rug from Persia, an *uchiwa* fan from Japan, an Egyptian vase of black and beige—displayed in her entranceway is too much. Brought together from all four corners of the world, these things should precede a house of stories and insight, whole afternoons spent discussing beliefs here and habits there, not riddles or confectionery. But Elias died fifteen years ago and left no children behind, nothing to keep Rita going. And so she stopped. Stopped travelling, stopped taking post-retirement calls from younger doctors anxious for her renowned advice. She stopped letting them look at her, too, and has sat as still as her artefacts ever since, growing older. Growing weaker. I feel stupid for not having seen her move to a hospice coming. It is a last resort in this country; when the temperature drops overnight, South Asian women can be seen pushing wheelchairs or supporting the shoulders of those they live with, care for, all around the neighbourhood. But Shehani is not enough for Rita anymore. Even with Atay here, her condition is worsening. Soon we will have no choice but to move her out of this flat, and then what will become of these things? Of these women, Shehani and Atay. There will only be room for one of them, my grandmother has proclaimed. I suppose the other will be deported.

I shut and bolt the bathroom door, turn around. The window, a square slant below the ceiling, is open. Beneath its grubby frame, I cock my head.

"Shehani, this is madness. You are dreaming," my grandmother says.

"No," Shehani insists, her voice an urgent whisper, "I am not."

"How can you be sure?"

"I *saw* her, I know I did. You must believe me."

Eliza grumbles something I cannot hear over the crickets.

"Please," Shehani begs her, "I am afraid."

A pause.

"We will talk in more detail about this," my grandmother says.

There is a sound beyond the bathroom door like footsteps. They are coming in, I realise, and I haven't even been to the toilet. No time. Teeth gritted, I flush it and suck my bladder up to my stomach. I will have taken too long otherwise, and they will think I was listening.

Shaking my needlessly washed hands dry, I open the door and freeze. There, behind the one out to the veranda, metres away from me, is Atay. Keeping her shoulders still, flat to the wall, she turns her head to look at me. My eyes widen as hers narrow. Her lips are colourless. She raises a finger to them as Shehani enters.

My grandmother is last inside. "Ah. My love," she says upon seeing me, "you are here. Come."

I walk towards her outstretched arms. Atay does not take her eyes off me. I can feel them with every step, though I am trying not to look so as not to betray her vantage point. As I pass by it I feel like I am transgressing again, crossing some boundary; she is watching and yet I will not tell on her because she has not told on me. Unless she has, I think. I panic; she has told Shehani and Shehani has told my grandmother. Eliza's grip is firm upon my arm.

Andreas and George have both finished their coffees by the time we sit down. Maria is on her phone. Rita is still moaning and so Shehani goes to settle her. No one else seems to have noticed that Atay slipped out of the room, or that she is slipping back in.

"So," my grandmother sighs, evidently exasperated by her confrontation outside. "Shall we go out for dinner tonight, all of us?"

"Oh no, I can't," Maria says in the softer, higher-pitched voice that I have noticed her affecting around her parents. Like she is not just *their* child but *a* child, still, too young to be scolded. "I have plans."

I look at her. "What are your plans?"

"I'm meeting my friends," she smiles, before ducking back onto her phone.

Andreas, I observe, has crossed one leg over the other and is fiddling with his shoe.

Once again, my grandmother sighs. "Okay. Well, just us then," she says, giving my thigh a pat and a squeeze.

"Oh. Erm, actually, I can't do tonight either."

At this, she withdraws her hand. "You can't?"

I shake my head. "But tomorrow . . ."

"Why not? Do you have plans tonight as well?"

The whole room has turned to look at me. Their collective gaze feels like my grandmother's grip all over again, all over *me*, crushing my windpipe. Do they suspect my indiscretion?

"I do have plans," I manage, "yes. I'm going on a date."

Nine

The bar Paris has selected for our date is impressive. In the afternoon, once it was cool enough, I walked there to see for myself the restored brick walls, the backlit bar, the bare bulbs strung on long black wires from the ceiling, metres up above bladeless fans. This I had never seen before: a hollow white hoop blowing cold air out—like bubbles if a child had their lips pressed to the other side—and yet there was no apparent generator. I could only assume the technology was expensive. The customers, too, looked lavishly put together, the older women with their hair swept gracefully back above diamonds, draped necklines; the young men in white shirts with the sleeves rolled up to match their high-heeled counterparts. Cigarette smoke drifted out, carrying with it elegant scents.

I lean to inspect my face in the bathroom mirror. Having returned home, showered and spent time agonising over various eye-shadows, I am no closer to feeling prepared. The lighting in here is too harsh for me to see what my makeup truly looks like, whether my pores are clogged with powder. Am I too shiny? I rush to my bedroom. It is kinder, this tall mirror, which leans on the wall across from the bed I have been sleeping in for over a week now. In it, in my black linen jumpsuit with its plunging V-neck and tight-buttoned waist, I look less overdone. Not underdone, I hope, as I turn to study myself over one shoulder and the fabric at my calves sways just-so. Done. No more and no less. I pull on some white trainers and lock up to leave.

It is still warm outside. My walk into town felt stickier, more strenuous than it has, I noticed earlier, and so it does again. Before long, July will come and I won't be able to manage it at all. Even with the fifteen, sometimes twenty-degree temperature drop overnight—we really do have desert weather here—high summer evenings are too hot. I will have to start driving. Learning how seemed pointless in London, where I was surrounded by trains and buses that came and went every two minutes. In this city there are no trains. The buses are unclean, unreliable and I was made to feel unsafe, the one time I got on one, by my music-blaring co-passengers and maniacal driver. Never again, Eliza decreed, to an eye-roll from my mother.

At the appearance of a green man, I step into the road and am almost hit by someone running a red light, then beeping at me. I want to shout after him but I am short of breath, and my overriding embarrassment has me hurrying to the far pavement, head bowed. I pause to collect myself. Four lines of traffic surge back to life and I think again of my wild bus ride. No one drives carefully here.

Thankfully, Paris's bar is in the pedestrianised part of the city, though I am still shaky when I reach it. The sky has darkened, more lights come on. Half the tables have already been taken by girls in their twenties and their dates. Not mine. I survey the space. He is nowhere to be seen.

People look at me as I accept a table towards the back, candlelit. It is in the non-smoking section, and I remember only once the waiter has gone that this might be a problem. I gnaw at my fingernail, gaze after him. 'Non-smoking' seems a generous term anyway; the bar lacks an entire wall so that one half of it can be called 'outside', though it is separated from the other, the 'inside', by a mere metal frame hung with plants. Lots of places stretch the smoking laws in this way here because lots of people smoke, I suppose. Like Beyza.

Her name in my head sends me shaking it side to side, as if to dislodge her from my memory. Who wants to think of an ex on a date? The first, perhaps, of many. Or not. My stomach churns. My relationship with Beyza is safe to think about because it is over, it can be known. Just not now. I am trying to build something new on nothing at all; I don't want to think about it. My external reaction to doing so catches me and I clear my throat, bow my face into my menu. Cocktails. I turn the page over. This seems to be what we are here for. Otherwise there are a few fine wines and one beer option for reluctant accompaniers. The whole thing feels very grown up to me, getting nicely dressed and placing orders based on a pretended knowledge of different mixers and grapes. Not at all like zipping a hoodie up to my chin and trudging through the park, in the rain, with Beyza. I grit my teeth. I don't know how to comport myself.

"Can I get you a drink?"

"Oh, yeah. Erm." I glance over my shoulder. "Actually, I'm still waiting for someone . . ."

Before I have asked for another minute, the waiter is gone. The girls at the next table look over again and I blush back down at my menu. Innocent Steel. I strain to focus on the item, a gin-based cocktail with violet and ginger. The next one down is the Undead, a blend of rums with citrus and spices. All the others contain at least one ingredient that I don't recognise. Everyone around me looks comfortable with their glasses in hand. I check the time. Paris is fifteen minutes late.

After ten more the waiter returns, a searching look upon his face. To steady my hands I order a Lemon Grove—a wine-based cocktail with mint and soda—which arrives in a long-stemmed glass and contains cuts of rosemary. I bend my neck to the straw, too afraid of dropping it to pick it up. It tastes sharp, good. So good that I only look up from it to check for the third, fourth, fifth time that Paris's message definitely said to meet him here, at eight-thirty, today.

"You must be careful," my grandmother's warning replays in my mind. She couldn't believe I would agree to go out with a man I had met so fleetingly. Perhaps he was a predator, she fretted.

"When and where are you going exactly? You must tell us, in case something happens."

But what if nothing happens? What if they stop by to see? Would that be worse than these strangers witnessing it? I am glancing constantly over my shoulder, wretched with wondering.

Then I am finished drinking, and it is close to twenty-past nine. I shunt my chair back, get the bill. Pay it. The same people who watched me walk in now watch as I walk out, still alone, redder-faced even than I was before. Now, though, it is with *anger* and self-consciousness, not nerves.

I decide I will get a taxi home to get away faster. Three of them are lined up at the square edge of the old city, but there is no one inside. I approach the booth across the road.

"What's your address?"

When I have given it, the man inside shouts to another who emerges from around the back, a can of beer in hand. He sees me waiting by the first taxi, as I have been instructed to, drains his drink in one and tosses the empty can underneath the car. I hear it crumple as we reverse over it, then set off towards my flat. I pull my seatbelt tight.

Halfway there, the driver's phone rings and he takes his hand off the gear stick to answer it. "I'm alright," he mumbles, "just driving."

The car in front of ours brakes and he swerves to avoid it just in time, stopping in the next lane halfway past the red light. An indistinct voice drones on in his ear. Whoever he is talking to, evidently, is unconcerned.

Ten

"Cheers!" Andreas bellows.

For the third time since our arrival at this restaurant, since we have had a first and second bottle of wine and plates of chicken, pork, goats' cheese, salad, pitas, dips and potatoes delivered and cleared, we raise our glasses. Me, my grandfather, Eliza, George. And for the third time, Maria does not join us. She looks down at the table, laid with a white cloth which is spattered now, and combs her fingers through her tangled hair.

"Maria," my grandmother says, "cheers."

She thrusts her drink at Maria's regardless, almost knocking it over with raw force. Anger, I realise, as she gulps back most of her glassful in one. Eliza has had enough of whatever strange thing is going on behind closed doors. I remember the one left open at Rita's, the snatch of conversation I overheard between her and Shehani, and I drink a good amount, too. The wine is pale, light. I take another gulp. Could Shehani really have been talking about me? When she claimed to have seen someone, a woman, doing something they shouldn't have been, something that made her worry. Did Atay tell her that she had seen me at the border? It is possible. Even if she did, though, why would Shehani claim to have been the one who saw me?

My glass lands unsteadily back on the table. Eliza's does, too, though more with violence than nervousness. Her dark eyes seem to be reserved for her daughter tonight. I release the air from my lungs. Perhaps it was Maria whom Shehani witnessed doing something unsavoury.

"Any dessert?" a waiter asks, his shirt bright white in the darkness.

"Erm." My aunt's fingers go taut between tendrils of her hair. She looks to the rest of us around the low-lit table.

"Yes," Andreas intervenes. He orders a portion of the complimentary sweet for everyone.

"You didn't even ask us," George twitters.

"You, okay. I should have asked," my grandfather admits. "But if we waited for Maria to decide, we'd be eating dessert for breakfast tomorrow."

He looks at me and descends into the delighted laughter of a child. I laugh along with him—and Maria, who is blushing—but never enough to keep up. And so I feel stiff and look down at my lap.

We all tuck in when dessert arrives, pink and dusted with cinnamon.

"Daniela, you must tell us. How was your date last night?"

I stop with my spoon halfway to my mouth. It hovers in the air along with Eliza's question, the creamy pudding upon it quivering. It hardly needs to be chewed, but I take my time gulping it down. "Actually, my date didn't happen."

"What?" My grandmother shakes her head as if unable to compute my words. "What do you mean it didn't happen?"

"Did he cancel?" Maria asks.

"Yeah. Well, not exactly." I look down at my plate. "I went there, and . . ."

"No," she exclaims, at my explanatory shrug.

"He didn't show up?" Eliza's eyes are wide.

Beside her, my grandfather yanks the napkin from his collar and throws it to the table. He has inhaled his dessert and his plate is gaping, as is he. "Unacceptable," he says, in English. Turning to my great grandfather, he resumes his first language, the language we have all been speaking, though he tuts as much as talks in it now. "Unacceptable," he reiterates, making absolutist gestures.

"Well," my grandmother says, after some moments of this, "it's better that he disappointed you than if he came and he was dangerous, I mean . . ." She shakes her head. "At least you know. He is not worth your time."

"That's true," Maria agrees.

I thank them both, though I am surprised my aunt doesn't have more to offer. At least three times she opens her mouth as though to add something, then gets interrupted or sits back again, simply thinking better of it. Why? I look closely at her watchful eyes, her forehead placid with refrain, still, at thirty-five. I remember her having a boyfriend in London who lived, along with many others from this island, in Camden. They were both studying, getting along well. Until they weren't. She never told me why and, come to think of it, she hasn't talked fondly of anyone since.

"Maria, are you seeing anyone?" I ask her, in the car on the way home.

Perhaps she is withholding simply because George is here, too, but I don't believe her giggling answer: no. Her eyes in the rear-view mirror are saying something else. They are *seeing* something else, I think, never mind the chaos of other cars on the road or the lights left on in shop windows long after they have closed.

Gravel crunches under the tyres as we ease into the parking beside our apartment building.

"Goodnight," George says, when we have climbed the stairs to the first floor.

He disappears into his flat while my aunt and I continue upwards. Past flats three and four, to doors numbered five and six.

"Here we are," I say. It is my turn to peel off.

With a gentle touch to my shoulder, Maria stops me. "I am sorry about your date."

"Oh. That's okay," I say. And part of me means it. There is a certainty to having been stood up, let down, an assurance that I know from my limited experience can never be felt when dating. If I could skip ahead to the dull drone of marriage, I would. To know for sure what every day would entail, who it would be spent with, where every holiday and misplaced pair of glasses would turn up . . . This second guessing is torture. But it is done for now, I tell myself, as much as I liked Paris, or liked the idea of him. I doubt he will contact me again.

"You should come out with me and my friends."

"What?"

"It's good to be distracted from these things," Maria persists, her brown eyes intent in the darkness.

"Yeah," I say, slowly.

She is right, it can be good to be distracted, and yet she remained quiet through our meal with George and her parents. Why not invite me out then? Why wait until now, when we are alone in this shadowy stairwell with the distant hum of a motorbike engine sending something in the lift shaft vibrating, and I can feel her breath like another soft touch upon my face? I think about flushing myself down the metal chute to escape my confusion, but Eliza has warned us all away from it. She had it attached to the side of the building when her father turned ninety, in spite of his good health. She was afraid he might not make it down the stairs one day. Then she took it up to see him and the doors opened onto solid wall. The many checks that have been done on it since have not reassured her.

"Will you come?" Maria asks.

There is another shudder behind me. I feel it in my bones and nod just as haltingly.

"Goodnight then," she says, and disappears up the stairs to the invisible fourth floor.

Hers is the only flat above mine, above all of ours. I stare after her with my key in my hand, wondering what goes on up there long after the door has clicked shut.

Eleven

A week later I am back in front of my bedroom mirror, agonising as if Paris has invited me out on another date. Unsurprisingly, he has not. My aunt, however, has told me in advance that her friends are hiring a boat for the day, and that I am welcome to throw on a swimsuit and join them if I would like. My bikini top is nothing fancy, two flat black triangles that tie around my neck and back. I have never felt drawn to the frills and padding that smaller girls seem to be. My breasts are shapely enough that they can carry themselves. It is my waist that could be, should be, slimmer. Teeth gritted, I turn side-on to the mirror. Then, with my high-waisted bottoms hitched right up to cover my stomach, I pull on a black kaftan and set out to meet Maria. My flip-flops snap down every step.

"Hallo," she says, when I have shut myself in the car beside her with a misjudged slam.

The interior smells, as it always has, of bubblegum and cigarettes.

With the air conditioning on full blast we drive off from our apartment building, out of our residential maze of one-way streets and down the main road. It splits into two lanes ahead of some traffic lights, one for the highway towards the coast and one for the city centre. The traffic has slowed right down. We wait to turn, inch forwards. And don't.

I frown. Maria is still humming along to a pop song that I must have heard ten times since my arrival, always on this radio station. The traffic in this direction has thinned, allowing her to speed onwards to the next set of lights. Confident. Perhaps she hasn't missed the exit, I think, turning to face the front in my seat. Perhaps she is taking us out of the city another way. But what other way?

"Where exactly is this boat?" I ask her, as we roll over a speed bump onto a narrow road of golden houses, all weathered walls, peeling shutters and splintering balconies.

She stops for someone coming round an even tighter corner before driving deeper into a part of the city I do not know. The roads become wider again, the buildings sparser. Her keys jangle in the ignition.

"Maria?"

She indicates right. We bank towards a skeletal metal warehouse stocked with cars and she names a place I have never been, though I have heard my grandfather call it home many times. A place that makes the air conditioning blast louder in my ears. A place on the Other Side.

"Can you stop?"

"What?"

71

"The car, stop the car. I feel sick." Even as I say this, I don't know if it is true. It might be. The sight of the crossing point, us heading straight towards it, is dizzying. Maria can't pull over soon enough. With my hand braced on the door, I stumble out next to a petrol station.

"Wait," she calls after me, "Where are you going?"

"I can't come with you," I call through the thick of the fumes. I throw the door shut and wave her on.

Craning to look at me, she rolls down the passenger window. "At least let me take you home."

I shake my head. The bubblegum and cigarette smell of her car—which once was comforting, familiar—now seems hazardous. At the thought of breathing it, I back away. "I just need to sit down for a bit. My head hurts. I need a coffee."

"We can get one on the way."

"No," I tell her, "I'll find somewhere to sit down here. You go. I'll be fine."

Maria hesitates. Another car comes up behind hers and she tries to reverse out the way of the entrance, but there is not enough space. "Call me when you get home," she concedes at last, and drives off.

I duck back down the narrow road and walk to where twenty stacked barrels cut it short. The wall. Dust settles between it and I as the car revs away, then fades into noiseless obscurity. I can hear my breath like I have been running, and feel the cling of sweat to my kaftan. My *kaftan*. My heart drops in time with my chin as I look down at myself. This is hardly urban attire. Flip-flops cracking, I approach the barrels. They are green-and-white-painted, secured in place by tarp and chicken wire. Some way off, a siren wails. I look over my shoulder. There is no one out in this neighbourhood, no residents because half the houses are collapsing, abandoned, and no soldiers because their next station is further along. My shoes fall silent as I reach out, touch a hand to the hard border. My fingers come away grimy, as if I have picked up an old coin; I lift them to my nostrils and they smell like it, too. Like rust and cold, the depths of a thousand pockets.

I don't go beyond the wall as my aunt has, but tread along it, wide-eyed, until I come to another crossing point. This one is in the pedestrianized part of the city, where I found myself last week. My skin prickles at the memory. Still, nothing has happened to make me think that Atay has revealed this yet.

The last establishment on our side of the border is a kebab house sardonically named The Berlin Wall. Following my nose, I take a seat outside and watch people cross over one way, the other. Several of them look local. This is a done thing now, I know, plenty of people live and work on opposite sides of the wall. Plenty more cross over just to fill their cars with petrol since it is so much cheaper on the Other Side. There are annual prizes awarded to the best bi-communal businesses now, to encourage goodwill. That's progress, I think, that's great.

Two tattooed men enter our side and with a grimace, I put down my menu.

So why can't I stomach it?

This question bothers me as I watch a man speaking our language, the language of The South, hold his phone away from his ear to show his documentation, cross the border and then keep speaking. Loudly, as if the voices around him haven't changed. This language is not the dominant one anymore, not where he is, just metres away from me. He shows no signs of noticing, and this only bothers me more. *Why*?

"Can I get you a drink?" a waiter asks.

"Some water, please. Thank you."

I sit back when a glass arrives, condensation trickling down its side. I sigh. I think, perhaps it is because I am an outsider after all. Unlike my aunt, I did not grow up here. I have not seen the nonviolent cohabitation of the modern everyday with my own eyes. Instead, I have heard my grandparents' stories of the invasion and of hardship, and so my perception is skewed. Perhaps we are all more protective of the things we love but cannot see; we feel any threat to them more keenly because of our powerlessness to stop it. The longer he lived abroad, the more furiously my father spoke out against 'the regime'. But that might have nothing to do with his having emigrated at all. It might be the result of his being an *imm*igrant, clinging tighter onto issues that made him an insider elsewhere because he was not one in England.

But did Maria do that, in her time as a foreign student? I don't think so. Perhaps their difference in attitude is generational. Running my finger down the tattered spine of my menu, I remember Jason hoisting me up into their parents' storage room, showing me the old toys and schoolwork they had kept. After the invasion, his exercise books had been given to him with that fateful date and the order 'never forget' stamped across their covers. These stamps looked faded to me, years after the fact, but they were not in the minds of the children who had carried their message to and from school every day. Hearing my father's friends talk taught me that. The covers of Maria's workbooks, meanwhile, given to her fourteen years later, were blank.

I take a long sip of water. The reality stands. Anyone young and open-minded enough to accept the change hardly talks about it at all—they don't remember the unrest—for they are too busy living their lives, hiring boats across the border. The sea is supposed to be beautiful there, pure blue. I know this because Andreas has told me how much he misses it, how no sand will ever feel so soft or warm beneath his feet as it did on the beach that was torn away from him, as if by the tide before a tsunami. His daughter, meanwhile, has only pleasant memories of that place, which she does not bother sharing because 'pleasant' is uneventful. She is not scarred by anything that has happened to her there; she just takes her passport and goes when she wants to. Another day at the beach. What is there, really, to report back about that?

If I had grown up here, I might be more relaxed about it, too. But I did not. I *am* not. I can't forget the hole in my grandmother's life or the hurt on my grandfather's face when the subject comes up, not as I close my eyes and gulp back the rest of my water. Not as I stand and start walking, eyes fixed on the crossing point, away from The Berlin Wall and towards this other one. Not even as I join the line, this time in earnest, can I put their anguish out of my mind. But perhaps, I think, drifting as though in a trance towards the soldiers and their guns, I can begin to understand it.

Palms sweating, I show my identification and cross over to the Other Side.

The Buffer Zone

Twelve

There is a green line cutting across one hundred and eighty kilometres of this island, or thereabouts. Like someone came along with a coloured pen to draw lines through another person's essay, crossing out what they did not like and leaving no helpful comments in the margins to suggest what might read better.

In the city where I live, these lines are drawn between beautiful buildings in decay. Soldiers hunch over the fraying wooden balconies on one street and watch over the next, where a rearing tangle of bushes will have grown. They let empty beer bottles and cigarette butts fall from between their fingers, knowing that they will not cause those who live here more upset than they already feel. They *cannot*.

Some of these houses are still owned by the people they were before the invasion. Some have lost their gardens to the Green Line, which stops dead at their back doors. If these are opened again, their owners risk being shot at by the soldiers on the Other Side, who watch us from the balconies they seized, guns in arms. My grandmother has a friend who cannot stand to look out her kitchen window at the wooden furniture that has been rained on, sun-bleached and pecked at by burrowing insects and birds in the years since she has set foot out there. She gardened, before the invasion. She kept her pots and beds well watered and organised until the attack was launched, the lines were drawn. They all spilled into each other and withered and died and were superseded by nameless weeds, then vines, so now she cannot tell if anything she planted remains. She wants to tear everything up by the roots. She wants to cast out that ghastly table and chairs, where she used to sit and catch her breath between raking up beds of soil, but she cannot. Nor can she afford to move. And so her back door stays locked, and her kitchen grows darker in the shade of the overgrowth.

In other areas the lines are further apart, the space between them not metres but kilometres wide. As jagged as a razor blade jerked from its course, the one marking the limits of the northern territory was drawn at the dirty boots of the men who took it, as was that penning us into The South. The UN stepped in to record both after the ceasefire. The space between them, the buffer zone, gnashes from coast to coast, uninterrupted in all but a few places. A former resort town controlled by the belligerents' military. A British Army base, which some of us speed through just to slap notes saying 'I don't recognise you' against our car windows when we are pulled over, then keep driving. Acres of the land are farmed—inhabited, even—inside specified Civil Use Areas. These we are allowed to come and go from freely now. The UN has pledged to work towards 'a return to normal conditions', very nobly. But we still need authorization to enter those other areas, those towns and villages we lived in, left to rot, otherwise they will 'respond'.

On both sides of this Green Line, there is bloodshed. There is family, hope, pain, sweat. There is one coffee shop opposite another, their petty rivalry mithering on in the shadow of this one. There is love, there is sex. There is endless regret. There are people who did not ask for this, any of it, who only want to live in peace.

And between our two sides, there are flowers. Pursed red tulips, beaming chrysanthemums, swooning crown anemones in every pencil box shade, white-flowering wild garlic, bushes of prickly broom with their tangling shocks of yellow and the whiskered petals of myrtle shrubs. Despite all the destruction these plants have continued to grow. They have grown stronger than ever without human interference, and they were tough to begin with, brambled and coarse. They had to be, in this climate. Everything does.

And yet they bloom, into the most unlikely kind of beauty.

Thirteen

"I was surprised when you messaged," I admit.

Paris inhales deeply as he lights his cigarillo. "Why?"

"I don't know. Do you know of any couples who kept dating after one of them stood the other up?"

At this, he smirks and I feel my shrug turn from cool to self-conscious, my shoulders creep up to shield my burning ears. The sun has gone but the temperature is still high, the space around us dotted with the same bladeless white fans it was the last time he invited me to this bar, like breathing holes in a box. Of course the last time he invited me to this bar, Paris did not show up. I waft the neckline of my linen jumpsuit away from my chest. Same jumpsuit. Same day of the week. A complete do-over, he insisted. I could have said no. I could have saved myself the trouble, the time, though that would have made him look stupid. And now? By giving him this second chance that he does not deserve, am I making myself appear any less foolish?

"Maybe not." Paris exhales smoke. "But we never know anything until we try it, right?"

Ice ricochets around a metal shaker behind the bar. When it stops, the sound of Green Day resumes like silence, jaded with laughter from the many tables around us. Movement draws my eye.

"No thanks," I say to the cigarillo Paris offers me. I hope he doesn't think less of me. I have dressed deliberately, as I did last time, with our environment in mind so as to look good in it, natural. Native, actually, in head-to-toe black. I wanted him to look at me and think that I belonged here, with him. I want a reason to feel sure of it myself. "So," I muster, digging my toe into the terrazzo floor under our table, "where were you the other week? What happened?"

"Let's see." Paris leans in on his elbows, points his second cigarillo at me and frowns. "I got held up, and you sat here. For how long?"

"I don't know. An hour, maybe," I say, taken aback.

"An *hour*?"

"Yeah."

As if hearing for the first time about someone else's poor treatment of me, he tuts. "And then what?"

"I finished my drink and took a taxi home," I murmur, blinking in bafflement at his creased brow and cocked head. I shake mine. "But that doesn't matter. *I* meant to ask *you*. Why couldn't you make it? Or call me."

"Life only moves forwards, right?" Paris says, once again with that glint in his eyes. Before I can respond, he taps his cigarillo into the thin metal ashtray between us and opens his menu. "Anyway, now that you mention drinks. What did you have last time? Anything you'd recommend?"

83

I stare at him over the top of it, leather-bound. Is he trying to be funny? "Yeah," I say, the moisture evaporating from my mouth, "the Lemon Grove. It was nice."

"Two of those, please."

A waiter I hadn't noticed sweeps our menus off the table, allowing Paris to lean in again. A silver chain teases down his shirt. On it will hang a cross, undoubtedly; every Orthodox child is given one by their godparents before they are baptised. I feel the plunge of my V-neck keenly. Born abroad to a mother whose core principle was freedom, my neck was left bare. I could choose whether I wanted to be baptised when I was older, she told my father. She doesn't understand that here, now, being a member of the Church is more about culture than belief. Perhaps I wouldn't choose to attend the service every week, but few people do and they still wear their crosses. Now there is this triangle of naked skin pointing, singling me out as other, again.

Paris catches me looking and fingers his chain, thoughtfully. My embarrassment turns to a blush. Despite his failure to attend our first date, despite his deflection on this one and every alarm bell in my head ringing high and clear so I can hardly stand it, his nearness compels me.

"So, Daniela." His eyes are bright through the smoke from his mouth. "What do you do for work?"

"I actually don't have a job yet. I just came here from England."

"Oh, you're still a student. Cool. You went to university in London?"

"No." The thought of my mother's disapproval renders my voice a mumble. "I didn't go to university."

Paris raises his eyebrows.

"My father did. Do you know Goldsmiths? That's in London." I am babbling now, turning as red as if I have never encountered confusion like his in response to this admission. Doesn't everyone go to university these days? What drama or defect stopped me? I clear my throat. "Anyway. He meant to come straight back, but he met my mother and ended up staying."

"Your mother is English?"

"American. She was there to study as well."

"Wow." Paris sits back. Candlelight catches the scar above his left eye, glistening white. "So you're from England."

"Well." I tip my head from side to side. "Not exactly. I was born there, but . . ."

"That explains the eyes." He fixes his upon mine and I feel them widen, forget my indignation as he leans closer, and covers my hand with his palm. "They are stunning."

"Two Lemon Groves?"

"Thanks."

I fumble to catch my breath. Paris has released me, but my heart is still beating hard.

"Cheers," he says, "to second first dates."

We touch glasses, sending our rosemary sprigs bobbing.

"And how about you?" I ask. "What do you do?"

"I work in security," he says, extending an arm to put his drink down.

My eyes go to his bicep. I picture him stationed outside a tall building in a top that accentuates its curve and the effortless gold of it, like something touched by a mythical king. Then his gaze shifts and mine follows it, to a darker-skinned man in a branded blue T-shirt, too big for him, shuffling inside. He is carrying his motorcycle helmet in one hand, showing his weary face.

"Oh. And I pick up some of that once in a while," Paris adds, referring to the delivery driver without so much as a nod. "Just if I want some extra cash, you know. It's not paying my mortgage." He stubs out his cigarillo. "Anyway. I let you down last week. Let tonight be about you."

He is deflecting again, I know he is, and still this makes my heart melt into my stomach. With stacked boxes in hand, the man in blue hobbles out again.

"Okay," I say. Even though I don't know what a night that is 'about me' should begin to look like. Here is this older boy, with a job in security and security in his job, enough that he can have a mortgage and a life here in this city that is all his own, fixed. He is self-assured to the point of cocky, grinning as he asks guiding questions that might help me figure it out. He sees something in me, I think, like Beyza did. He must do. I would like to find out what that is for myself.

"Good," Paris says. And he lights another cigarillo.

Fourteen

"Daniela, my love."

I take a deep breath of bougainvillaea. Its scent is surprisingly muted, truer to the tiny white flowers inside its pink bracts so my nostrils flare for more to grasp, to steady me on the steps up to Rita's veranda. This is the first time I have seen Eliza since I crossed over to the Other Side, since I crossed her and Andreas and everyone else in my dear, wronged family. Except Maria, of course. Maria is the exception to everything, it seems.

"Good morning," I bid my grandmother.

I do not look directly at her as she steps aside, opening her palm as wide as Rita's front door in invitation. "Please, come in."

Head bowed, I do as she says.

"Hallo," Shehani greets me.

She is brighter today, standing tall over my great aunt's seat at the head of the coffee table, back to her beaming self. She is back at her cooking, too; the smell of bitter herbs and curry powder soaks through from the kitchen. I gulp back saliva. This is the first time since my arrival that she has woken up and gone to work on an elaborate meal. She used to do it once a week, I am certain. I relished the taste of these aromas in the air.

"Shehani," I say, "isn't it your day off? Where is Atay?"

"Atay takes Sundays off now," my grandmother informs me, collapsing onto the sofa with a huff. "Shehani takes Mondays instead."

"Yes." Shehani smiles less broadly at the mention of her co-worker's name.

I can hardly blame her. Remembering the Sunday I saw Atay in town sends a sensation like fingertips trailing up my spine, and the shakiness comes back into my voice when I think of the last time I was in town at all. I was abroad.

I try to change the subject before the guilt can overcome me, before anyone can deduce it from the way that I look different, smell different, am different. I must be. I am just not certain how. I am just not certain, still. "Where is everyone else?" I ask.

Aside from myself, my grandmother, Shehani and my great aunt gurgling as she is spoon-fed a mush of oats, the room is empty. Dark as ever, droning with fans.

"Have a seat." Patting the cushion beside her, Eliza answers, "Andreas is meeting some of his ex-colleagues for coffee. My father went up to the village last night, so he will stay there until later on."

I nod. "And Maria?"

At this, Shehani looks up and the spoon clatters from her hand onto the marble floor, shrilly. Blushing apologies, she rushes to clean it up, fetch a new one, smooth her polished black hair and get on with feeding Rita who is groaning, unsettled.

89

"Maria? I don't know. She had some plans, something," my grandmother says.

Her scraggly brows are just two of countless lines across her forehead from all the puzzling and pestering she has done over the decades. Where are you going? Who with? When will you be back? She will have asked all these things of my aunt, and folded the answers away into yet more creases that I hadn't noticed before this year. Still, she cannot account for everyone. Does it soothe her, I wonder, to control the knowledge of our whereabouts in this way? To choose who gets to know what when, as she was not allowed to when her mother went missing?

She waves a hand. "Anyway. I spoke to your parents. Today is your mother's birthday, you know."

My stomach turns over. Yes, I do know.

"She told me they haven't heard from you since you left."

"Erm." I take a moment, take a sip from a glass of water that I can only hope was put out for me.

Eliza does not drop my gaze.

I take another sip, and another one.

"Sorry to interrupt. Shall I make some coffee?" Shehani asks. She has straightened and is holding Rita's empty breakfast bowl at her hip. It is lime-green, plastic, like one that a child might eat from.

I accept her offer with a hoarse voice. I have been avoiding my parents, it's true. They were so concerned about me moving

90

here and not settling into a degree or a career. A relationship, even.

"You have nothing stable in your life," my mother lamented before I left.

I know, I said then. I know it now. But I needed to explore this side of myself, and still do. I think it hurt her that I felt the stronger pull to my father's foreign background, growing up, and not hers. I don't know why this was. Perhaps it was the otherness of the features I inherited from his side that meant I could not ignore it. If you looked at an American person next to an English one, you wouldn't know the difference until they opened their mouth, yet people in England often looked twice at me before I said a word. Especially when I was out with my father, or with Beyza. I did enjoy some aspects of my alienness, like speaking a second language. It's fun, knowing that you can say almost anything about anyone, and they will not understand you. It makes you feel like you are part of something, exclusivity being inclusivity. And vice versa; when visiting my family in America— this happened rarely due to the expense—I only ever felt like an outsider, on the back foot, not knowing my way around.

But am I so much better integrated into my father's country, really, now that I am here to stay?

"I need to call them," I say, "I've just been busy. You know. But I do need to call and tell them I dropped my CV off at a few places yesterday. They'll want to hear that."

"You did?" Eliza sits back, wide-eyed. "Why didn't you tell me you were ready to start working? I would have arranged something for you . . ."

"No," I snap.

My grandmother blinks; I see her in the corner of my vision but still do not look straight at her. I can't, not when I have committed what she will surely view as the ultimate act of betrayal. All she does is try to help me.

"Thank you," I add, softly.

I finish my coffee as fast as I can and go back upstairs.

The door echoes shut behind me. Setting the ceiling fan in motion, I sit down at the table pocked with ring marks and rub at one as I might a blemish on my skin. My phone rings out and I stand up again, start pacing, anticipating my mother's wrath.

"Well. This is a surprise."

"Hi," I bleat into the microphone, thinking of the nine missed calls I saw next to her name before dialling. "I'm sorry . . ."

"Not to worry." Her words sound pinched, unreflective of their meaning. "It's just nice to hear from you. How are you getting on over there?"

Dropping my fingernails from my teeth, I look around. Everything under the fan is very still. I, too, I realise, have turned rigid with worry. "Fine. Good. I'm so sorry," I say again.

And again she dismisses my apology. "You've had a lot on, I'm sure."

"Is that Dani?" my father's voice sounds, in the background.

"Yes, our daughter. Remember her?" I can practically hear Deborah raising her eyebrows above her staunchly levelled voice. She is trying her best, telling me, "He wants you to call him back later. He's just on his way out to the supermarket."

"Okay," I say, as if I don't know that Jason waits until they have fought and he wants to get out of the house to go shopping. I sit back, remembering my desire to hear my stomach growl into an empty fridge. Then Shehani, who had to abandon her daughter because that was all she had known. I close my eyes.

My mother's tone remains taut throughout our conversation, but instead of directing her bitterness at me she grumbles about other things. The weather in London is awful, she says, the school where she works won't close for the so-called summer for another three weeks and she is beyond fed up with it. My father had better hurry and book their flights out here soon. She needs a change of scene.

"Happy birthday," I say, when at last she has exhausted herself.

"Huh. Well, that was better than Maria's effort. She sent me a text. *Enjoy your day*," my mother sneers. "Typical."

By now she has talked herself deep into her cynicism and I am leaning forwards, leaning backwards, crossing one leg over the other and uncrossing it again.

I frown. "Why is that typical?"

"Because. She doesn't wish anyone a happy anything, does she?"

"Doesn't she?" I had never noticed.

"She can't. It's against the rules."

"What rules?"

A voice sounds in the background. My father's again, sharp with warning. He says something I do not hear, something urgent, before my mother tells me that she has to go and hangs up her phone.

I stare at mine in disbelief.

Fifteen

I have not seen my aunt since she invited me out on the boat with her friends, since I jumped out of her car at the side of the road and told her to go on without me. I still feel bad about that. I am also still curious about the circles she moves in, and so I ask if I can join them another time, now that I am feeling better.

"Of course," she says. "How about Saturday?"

"That would be nice."

"Okay, perfect. Wear something you can walk in."

I have settled on a pair of olive-green cargo trousers and a black top, the straps of which are taut over my shoulders, sealing me, airtight, inside. For the first time since my arrival, even my feet are sealed away. There are too many snakes, where we are going, to risk serving them up on open soles.

Side by side in her car smelling of bubblegum and cigarettes, my aunt and I leave the city. Our side of it, this time. We take *our* highway past *our* shopping mall, past a clamour of houses that could only afford to be built so pillared and tall next to the unpleasantness of it, before *our* countryside fills the windows. Flat, cracked earth to either side. I think of the endless rain in England and wish they could spare us some. July and August, our danger months, are looming. There will be fires. There will be droughts. There will be temperatures upwards of forty degrees

Celsius, daily, which my great grandfather will monitor with a grave face. A floor below him, Rita will sag through another year without air conditioning while her carers pant and sweat. I don't know how they do it. One summer, when I was a child, almost one-hundred containers of explosives went off at a naval base. A tragedy, people called it, a shock. Devastating. But those explosives had been stored, beneath the blazing sun, in metal shacks next to a power station. My father was inconsolably outraged. Every day, each area was rationed one hour of electricity. That meant one hour of air conditioning, cooking, television. Per *day*. My memories are of holding battery-powered fans up to my face, of my mother sitting with her feet in buckets of water while her in-laws argued politics, and of chasing the power around the city. We were revolutionaries, my parents and I. We went from coffee shop to coffee shop, working out which ones had their fans in motion by the many cars parked outside. Sometimes we got lucky. Other times we retreated home with aching heads, dry mouths and only warm water to drink; without the fridge to bottle it in, tap water hit our glasses as hot as the sun on the pipes.

Maria turns the volume up on the radio. "I like this song."

Another number from the late nineties or early two-thousands. The same few of these get played on rotation here, as though they have just been released.

"Me too," I say.

Music blaring, we drive until the earth slants away from us; gnarled stems splay out at horizontals to the road, which curves up to the foothills of the island's tallest mountain range. We stop at an old mill town, where Maria has arranged to meet her friends for a riverside walk and some lunch. It is cooler here than in the city, I notice, stepping out of the car, and greener in this valley than it is atop the mountains themselves, thanks to the water supply. It is beautiful, almost lush.

We cross the road towards a ramshackle restaurant.

Inside, the ceiling is low and two of the four walls are heavily wood-clad. It is bright and airy with the other two open, one to the winding street and the other to a balcony overlooking more trees. At the smell of slow-cooked meat, hunger pounds its fist on the table of my stomach. I am glad of the babbling of families and the barking of a senior lady at her wait staff. She narrows her eyes when we tell her we are here to meet some friends.

"There they are, over there," Maria says, waving. She stops at a long table, separated from the toilet door only by a squat fridge. "Everyone, this is Daniela. Dani, meet Lim, Elena, Eziamaka and Rose."

"Hallo . . ."

I greet each of her friends in turn, then stand back and observe them. "Nice to meet you all," I say, to four people I might never have grouped together.

A waiter brings us some menus. I sit down opposite my aunt, with my back to the fridge and her friends to my left.

"So you've just moved here?" Lim asks me, in accented English.

"A couple of weeks ago, yeah."

"She still has the novelty," Maria smiles, unrecognisably bolder in the presence of her friends.

"No novelty," Lim prods her, "This is a good place to live. I love it, and I have been here . . ." She searches her broad forehead with stubby-lashed eyes. "Seventeen, eighteen years?"

"Wow. Where were you before?"

Everyone else remains quiet while I ask this, gently. They must already know. I banish the memory of a walk my parents took me on around a Sussex village, when a man asked my father where he was from and sniffed at the answer. How unusual, he remarked, evidently a local unused to diversity. My father stormed the rest of the path in silence, paces ahead of my mother and I. Hurt. Here, in this company, I suppose I might look like the local, despite having just arrived. It is not for my benefit that Maria's friends are speaking English. I feel acutely aware of the hum of the fridge, of causing anyone to feel the way that I did in England.

"China," Lim says, unfazed.

Relief empties my lungs. She will never go back even to visit, she adds, because there are too many people where she is from, it is too competitive and stressful; she prefers the pace of things here. Travelling with her today is Elena, who looks my age or older but apparently has just turned fourteen. I stare at the girl, trying to figure out what she is doing with this middle-aged woman who is not her mother, who cannot be her friend, until Lim mentions that she is just 'playing parent' for the day.

"For my friend." She says 'my friend' with the same quiet, smiling ambiguity that Maria does so often.

Elena smiles dully in return, then looks away. Excluding myself and my aunt, she is the only one among us who speaks the language of this island fluently, though she is so quiet you would not know it. The others are Eziamaka from Nigeria and Rose from the Congo, both women with exuberantly rich dark skin. Eziamaka must be in her thirties, with a broad smile, round shoulders and breasts that are just beginning to drop. Rose is thinner-lipped, thinner all over. She opens her mouth only slightly to speak and chuckles soundlessly into her lap. At first I think she is younger than Elena, but it transpires that she is older than I am: twenty-four.

"Are you ready to order?"

"Erm, I don't know." My aunt cranes to see down the table. "Are you ready, Rose? Eziamaka? Lim, is Elena ready?"

"I am," I say, when she turns to me.

This doesn't seem to matter. Maria's friends are as indecisive as she is, I observe as they deliberate. I am used to her taking some time to decide what she wants when we go out with our family, saying at first that she is stuck between four things, then stuck between three, then two and then blurting out one when a waiter asks for her order. But with her friends similarly hesitant, this process takes longer than ever. We have to ask for 'another minute' three times before having our menus cleared.

"Again," Eziamaka chortles, the second time we dismiss our waiter.

"You choose for me," Maria says, sagging against one of her majestic shoulders.

"How shall I choose for you? I can't even make up my own mind."

They collapse into more laughter and I smile, politely, though I feel somehow that I am not in on the joke. The waiter comes round again, and again they say that they need more time, they are undecided. I, too, start to question myself, right down to salad or fries. But the group is welcoming, its members good at smiling and listening. Lunchtime is pleasant.

"So you came here from England," Rose says to me, afterwards.

With the sun on our backs, we have walked through town to the old mill, now an impressive hotel. A dirt path starts at its feet and snakes alongside the river, shaded by trees. We have followed it around corners and over bridges, and stopped on a ledge overlooking a waterfall. There is the sound of the water folding into itself, birds cheeping, twigs snapping as Elena climbs down the bank and across some protruding rocks, while Lim takes pictures for her mother. Some moments ago, Maria and Eziamaka sat down on a nearby bench. I heard them laughing, loudly, though I didn't know what at. Perhaps they were the reason I could not hear Rose coming up behind me.

Looking at her, I search for signs of the resentment I often fear Shehani feels towards me; I grew up in London and chose to come here, to squander that opportunity. Even my great grandfather is frustrated by this. Is Rose, too, unable to understand it? Probably, I think, though she is impossible to read, her gaze fixed on the river below us.

"Careful," Lim calls, as Elena slips back a stepping stone, "Your mother will charge me your damages."

Elena laughs and continues to climb.

"What is it you want to do? What is your plan?" Rose persists.

Her voice, though probing, is soft. And yet I can hear it clearly; it is as though everything else has stopped.

"Honestly, I don't know."

As these words leave my mouth, I see Eziamaka picking her way down to stand with Lim. I look over my shoulder and there is my aunt, her head cocked to listen to me. A breeze blows in between us.

"I didn't know what I wanted or where I belonged," Maria tells me, when we get home, "but these people, my friends, really helped me."

In the echoing stairwell outside my flat, I shake my head. "But you did know," I say, urgency brimming from nowhere behind my eyes. "You always knew. You wanted to be an artist. What happened?"

"Knowing what you want does not mean you will get it," she smiles, sadly, "and learning that is hard."

Indeed. The principle that underpins my entire belief system, my struggle for certainty, has been razed to dust. I search her, imploring.

"But it helps to have support. If you're interested, let me know."

With this, she scribbles an address down on a scrap of paper from her bag and presses it upon me. Still I stare at her, blankly. Her feet sound on the stairs, her door shuts. My fingers feel so numb holding the paper that I have to look down to check it is there. Then I see: the address is for a church.

Sixteen

The next day, a Sunday, clouds are strewn across the sky. I rub the sleep from my eyes with a grimace. A break from the unobstructed sun should be welcome, but these clouds are fluffy and white, not the kind that will release moisture so much as trap it in the air, make it harder to breathe. When the temperature gets up I will feel as though I am soaking in a bath, and sweat enough sitting still that I might just have climbed out of one. This humidity is rare here, at least. Leaving the shutters half down, I retreat to bed with my phone.

'Jehovah's Witnesses', I type into Google.

It seems blunt, on the nose, a question made of a persuasion. But what I need is a blunt, on the nose answer. I know nothing of my aunt's religion except that it is a denomination of Christianity. And, since I looked up the address she gave me, that their places of worship are called Kingdom Halls; they are different from our Orthodox churches.

Jw.org is the first website that comes up. 'We worship the one true and Almighty God, the Creator, whose name is Jehovah', it states. 'We recognize the Bible as God's inspired message to humans . . . We base our beliefs on all 66 of its books . . . We recognize that parts of the Bible are written in figurative or symbolic language and are not to be understood literally . . .'

Scrolling further through the fundamentals, I come to a passage about the Kingdom of God.

'This is a real government in heaven, not a condition in the hearts of Christians. It will replace human governments and accomplish God's purpose for the earth', it says. Then, 'It will take these actions soon, for Bible prophecy indicates that we are living in "the last days"'.

I blink, horrified. This information is frightening and yet, flippantly, they give it like a weather forecast. Perhaps it is one, I think, glancing again at the searing blue sky. I want to wring those clouds out with my bare hands, but I am human. I can only hope and fear. Jehovah is said to possess all the power of the Trinity combined, and to have an entire government at His disposal. I have never heard of anything so organised or bureaucratic behind an afterlife. On Earth, our politicians are deceitful and contradictory; they choose wrongly or for the wrong reasons and rarely share a common vision. Meanwhile, Jehovah's administration presents harmony. Even in the face of apocalyptic uncertainty, they are steadfast.

I lie back against my pillows. I think of how unsettled and anxious Maria was in London, ten years ago, when she was trying to pursue art. Despite being set on the vocation, she had no idea how to secure it, no idea where to start. She was flustered, both overworked and unemployed, perpetually. Stretching her money as far as she could, she squeezed her work into exhibitions at obscure galleries, then onto the narrow backs of postcards to be sold in chocolate-box cafes, until at last she was running the arts and crafts sessions for after-school clubs. I can see this now, looking back with adult eyes. The fitful decline. I can understand how, unable to live with the instability anymore, my aunt gave up on her dream. Perhaps being fixed on one goal would not make life as easy as I had thought it might after all. But turning to faith, which is always there? Perhaps that is wise. Maria is as happy and at peace as I have ever seen her. So what is our family's problem with it?

Curious, I order a taxi and give the driver the address that my aunt gave me. In the rear-view mirror, I see his shaggy brows twinge before he drives off. He is silent. I fidget in the backseat seat and wonder whether I should just have given him the street name, and not mentioned the Kingdom Hall. Then I feel a tide of protectiveness over my aunt. Who is this man to judge anyone for their practices? I know that to be from this island is to be Orthodox, traditionally, but traditions are changing everywhere, becoming relics of the past as people come from all over to live side by side, however differently. No one should be outcast for their faith, anywhere.

Playing my driver at his silence, I stare stolidly out the window. He has slipped the traffic of the centre and is taking us down a long, wide road. It curves around an earthen ridge, tall enough that the city disappears behind it and I feel like we are miles outside. Then, the proof that we are not. I catch my breath. Our occupants' flag, carved into the mountain on their side of the metropolis. We are barrelling straight towards it—*into* it, I fear— it looks so large and looming that we must have crossed the buffer zone, unchecked. I have never seen it so close up before. We blare past a picture of a camera with a line through it, a sign that says 'Photography Prohibited' in two languages.

"Are we going the right way?" I ask, straining to keep the panic from my voice.

My driver grunts, then jerks the car off the first exit of a roundabout, away from the flag. I peel myself off the right-hand window and there it is: the Kingdom Hall. Relief floods my body. I pay the man and get out of his car.

My surroundings seem otherworldly and strange. Rather like the religion itself does, I suppose, in this country. The building is pale and flat-roofed, boxy, half of it being eaten from the bottom up by the ridge. Dust swirls at my feet. The heat is rising already, my lungs heaving with extra effort. Across the road is a miscellaneous row of warehouse-style shops selling used cars, paint and, bizarrely, surfboards. There are no customers in sight. The owner of the surf shop stands in his doorway, wearing a white vest. He takes long drags of his cigarette as he watches me, watches the church, as a police officer might a suspect. I glance at it once more through the iron railings. A sign says there will be a service at one o'clock today, as it is Sunday. Doubtless, Maria will be there. Should I accept her invitation? I am still unsure of my feelings on God, but perhaps she is right. Perhaps I would get some reassurance out of attending, even if only once.

With the surfboard salesman's eyes boring into my back, I begin to walk up the ridge. Slow steps, shallow breaths through my nose. This street lacks the shade of both trees and buildings, being part of the city, being at its precipice. At the peak of the ridge where no more shops block my view, I stop. Dust scatters across the road. There is that flag again, practically rippling. I feel it staring, daring me to blink and so I do not, until a passing car blows dust into my eyes. Then I continue down the ridge into the city.

Buildings spring up around me. Cars slow down or grind to a halt in traffic. It is all so big, so bustling, that I barely notice myself walking towards the centre, across the square, into the pedestrianised part of it. Overhead, the yellow and white flags dance like sunlight on some water's surface; I am submerged, knowing which way is up but not how to kick towards it. I smell cigarettes and grilling meat. I think of the flag on the Other Side and wonder if I am as close to it now as I was at the Kingdom Hall, even though I cannot see it from here. I see a wide white umbrella, people shuffling closer to its shade one at a time. Then it is my time. My ID is in my hand and someone is nodding, waving me through. I blink. For the second time, I am on the Other Side.

107

I have not thought about the first time since it happened. The fact that I came here, yes. I have thought about that guiltily, ceaselessly. But not the city itself, not what I saw or heard or smelled. I think I walked around it in such a state of dismay at my own crossing that I could not take in any detail; the city jangled so glaringly with my anxiety that no single part of it stood out to me from the haze. Nothing real. The one figment I do remember was of my own imagination: Beyza, on every street corner. I was sure I saw her, at the time. Her bow-shaped lips and soft yellow hands, her eyes thick with lashes and her teeth small when she laughed, like a child's. They were endearing. But they were not real, I tell myself, shaking my head from the fog that has overcome it again. I am here, alone, on the Other Side. I have been dreaming of her, but now I am awake.

And there she is.

Seventeen

"Dani," Beyza says.

There is that same rasp to her voice. At the sound of her saying my name, I remember the dark look that overcame her when anyone else referred to me this way. 'Dani', a classmate of ours would say, and Beyza would sulk as if this had not been my nickname for sixteen years. She wanted to have established it. She wanted to have a monopoly on it. Today, though, there is none of that. Her face is open. It is her head that is covered.

"I almost didn't recognise you," I stammer, as we draw apart from an awkward embrace. I don't say that this is because I have seen her before, not far from here, where the Other Side meets the edge of my imagination; I don't say that I distrust my own eyes. Instead I gesture to her hijab and admit, tentatively, "I've never seen you wear one before."

Beyza shrugs and the pond-green fabric pooling on her shoulders ripples. She is staying with her grandparents, she tells me, who feel strongly that she should. "Small price to pay to spend the summer here rent free."

"It must get hot though," I say.

She nods, wide-eyed. "And itchy. My hair's been going static underneath it all day. It's this humidity."

"God, yeah. Of course." I shift my weight from one foot to the other.

Beyza smooths a hand back from her hairline, eyes half closed, and I am reminded of the way she used to tip her head back in the shower, the way the water lengthened and glistened through her thick locks of hair, just like it did mine. Never mind the fact that when dry, hers was wavy and chestnut-brown while mine was line-straight, jet-black. We were the same, I thought, and she was beautiful.

I clear my throat. "So . . ?"

"How . . ?"

We laugh, haltingly, having opened our mouths at the same time to ask each other more questions, five years' silence filling questions. It happens again, we falter again, then fall quiet again.

Beyza looks at me. "Do you want to sit somewhere," she asks, "to talk?"

"Yeah." The word lights up a smile I wasn't aware of on my face. "Okay."

From the safety of her shadow, I look around. I am bolder in her presence, however surreal it may be. I am able to absorb my surroundings as I was not before. There are cats everywhere, just like on my side of the border. I smile at a pair curled up together before we round a bend and my face falls. I cannot breathe between the many shops in this narrow street, with their oppressive racks of branded clothes and bags and trainers bearing downhill at me, blocking out the blue sky. Fendi, Christian Dior, Dolce & Gabbana, men slouched on plastic stools out front and people pushing and pulling, bartering back and forth with words that ricochet off my ears and resound in my head. I cannot understand them, cannot understand anything except Beyza murmuring that we'll just slip through here, it's best I stay away from these items because they are fake and will only be taken off me at the border. Her warning heightens my alarm further so that I feel my ears shrinking up to the crown of my head, just as I did last time.

We reach the top of the hill and there, there are no more shops. The road widens, still cobbled, into quiet. Then coffee shops. I empty my lungs, feel my ears sink with them back to their rightful positions.

"Here," Beyza says.

She eases herself onto a swing that is suspended, at barstool height, outside a broad-bricked building. Acoustic guitar music floats from inside.

"Wow." The ropes of the swing opposite hers, too, are wrapped around with pink and white flowering vines. They bristle in my grasp; there is a creak as I heft myself up by them.

"Hallo, ladies," a waiter says, putting two drinks menus down in front of us. "How are you?"

Extending my smile to him, briefly, I turn over one of the menus. There are hot and cold coffee options, fresh juices, beers.

What will Beyza have? I hope she tells me outright so I don't have to look as meek and floundering as I feel by asking, emulating.

At the sound of her voice, I look up to see that our waiter has lingered to hear her answer.

"Good," she is saying, holding his gaze, "how are you?"

"Very well, thank you." He nods, a half-bow. "May I get you some water to start with?"

"Yes please," she says.

"No problem."

I stare after the boy with his faded-up and slicked-back hair. Was he flirting with her? He seemed oddly friendly. Beyza doesn't appear to have noticed this, nor does she comment on the fact that this is a nice place, and a coffee costs the equivalent of—I frown back at my menu—fifty pence. Can that be right? She picks at her chipped black nails and I am reminded of the poor maths skills that brought us together.

"Will you be here for a while then?" I ask her.

She lets her hands fall to the table. "Yeah. I've just finished uni, so. This is my last summer of freedom."

"Oh god." I grit my teeth. I have got to stop saying that, I think, catching sight of her hijab. But why? I am sure we both used to say it, and she was never offended before. Still, I correct myself, "*Right*. What did you study?"

"History and politics. At Canterbury Christ Church? I had a lot to do with that decision, as I'm sure you can imagine." An air of good-humoured resignation leaves her nostrils. "How about you?"

I shake my head, disguise a grimace. I know the stereotypes that surround the children of immigrants. I know that I am not living up to them. "I didn't do uni, actually. Just got a job straight after school."

"Lucky you," Beyza says.

I look at her. "Didn't you like your course?"

With her eyebrows alone, she shrugs.

"Or Canterbury?"

"I don't know. People go on about Canterbury, but I think it's kind of a postcard place. Nice for a day, or for a picture. Blank underneath."

Shy, I tuck my laughter away with my hair, behind my ears that feel rubbery for their lack of piercings; I could never decide if they would suit me. Beneath her hijab, I know, Beyza's are like ladders with rungs of silver from their lobes to their tips.

"What about the social side of things there? Did you," I release no breath with the word, "*enjoy* that?"

In an instant Beyza goes from sitting back, relaxed, to leering towards me. "What do you want?" she hisses.

The frame suspending us shrieks as I jerk backwards and my swing reacts, making me grab at the ropes. "I . . ."

"Quickly." She glances up.

113

"Oh," I breathe, at the sight of the waiter coming back with our water. "I'll just have an iced latte, please. Sorry. Thank you."

She translates and he talks back to her in the language they share, that I do not, while I empty my glass and refill it from the sweating bottle between us.

"What were you saying?" she asks, when he is gone. Her tone is as level as her gaze, as ever. She is placid until provoked.

I feel acutely aware of my knuckles, white around the ropes of my swing and so low down that my elbows must be jutting out at alarming angles. The vines tickle between my fingers. "I just asked," I repeat, slowly, "if you got much out of the social side, at least?"

Beyza does not break eye contact. We both know what I am truly asking, however awkward my phrasing, making me cringe. Did she make friends, like I did at sixth form? Did she get a new girlfriend or a boyfriend or sleep her way around the city? Her eyes are edged with black liner, her lashes flecked with mascara, her lips stained bold red. She came to this look early and has stuck with it ever since.

"I don't think I'll keep in touch with anyone in a big way," she says. "I mean, Pete lived in Canterbury. Still does."

Of course. Her on-off older boyfriend Pete, who she met online and was mostly 'on' with for weed and safe though uninspiring companionship. I remember now. Beyza spent her free time with him, she tells me, while other women in headscarves wheel their pushchairs past our table. She even moved into his studio for her third year, having become too red-eyed and reclusive for her housemates.

"Oh. So you were, like, a proper couple then," I say. I free my hair from behind one ear, tuck it back again. The vines rustle when I return my hand to the rope of my swing.

"We gave it a go," Beyza admits. "It was going well. Until I found out he was watching porn."

"Oh."

"All the fucking time, he was so disloyal." The light comes back into her eyes only when our waiter returns, with two coffees in cut crystal glasses. She thanks him warmly, then turns back to me. "Guys think that doesn't count as cheating, but it definitely does."

"Mmn."

I pull one of the drinks towards me and its ice cubes bob and clink. Recalling my own experience of Beyza's jealousy, I wonder whether this is true. Watching porn seems to me like a good way of *refraining* from cheating, a way for someone to satisfy their desires for something else, something new, without acting on them for real. But what do I know? I tear a strip of the paper wrapping off my straw clumsily, without freeing it, then try again. I have never caught a partner watching porn. Beyza has, and she seems certain. Perhaps she does know best.

"So is it over between you and Pete then? Really?"

"It is. Really, this time. I've decided. I'm not even going to go to him for weed when I'm back in England."

"Wow," I say, affecting amazement as I plunge the straw into my coffee. We laugh. "So what will you do next?"

"Oh, you know." Beyza sighs. "Get a job, settle down." Her brown eyes drift from the frame of our swing set to mine, and her face settles into a smile. "But not just yet."

Later, when I lie down to sleep, my head swarms with thoughts of Beyza and the way things used to be between us. My feelings are not rushing back, I try to soothe myself, it is natural to reflect on these things when you see an ex for the first time in years.

As if to prove this to myself after some further tossing and turning, I get up and stand in the midst of my darkened flat, phone in hand, staring at Paris's number on the screen. I could call him, but it is late. What would he think? What would I say?

'Are you awake?' I text him, eventually, something coy and non-committal that could lead to more, if I want it to. Or not.

Flustered with nerves, I let my phone clatter to the table and tear my way out to the balcony for some air. My head is pounding in time with my heart, my breaths coming quick and short. It is hours later than I am usually awake and pitch black outside; my flat faces a park on this side, so there are no city lights to be seen. Every few moments a car sighs, blocks away. There is the squalling of cats and one siren weaving its way through the stars above.

Then something splinters, a door from its frame. Someone bursts out of it, their breathing more ragged than mine. I look down. A curtain of hair. Hands bunched into fists. Bare feet pummelling first Rita's veranda and then the pavement beyond, until I cannot see the gasping girl they belong to anymore. Below me, a rectangle of light remains where the door has been left open. I stare out in search of Shehani until someone else closes it, soundlessly, and the light is gone.

Eighteen

"Good morning," my grandmother calls from Rita's veranda. "How are you?"

As I walk closer, she comes into view from behind the bougainvillaea, her black top and trousers a shadow of its vibrant pink.

"Good," I say. "How are you? And how is Shehani?"

The gate screeches shut behind me.

"I am well, my love. Everyone is well. Shehani, Atay . . . Rita," she adds with a regretful shrug, "is as well as she can be. And you, you are going somewhere?" She gestures to my tote bag.

The strap digs into my shoulder, weighed down by yet more copies of my CV. Pressed between every page is my desperation to get out of this building, away from my family with their questions and their feelings, which I know I will only hurt if I give truthful answers.

"Just into town." I muster a smile. Then, feeling my eyebrows cave inwards under Eliza's scrutiny, I retreat to concerning, "I saw Shehani last night. In the middle of the night, she ran outside crying. She didn't have any shoes on. I didn't see her come back . . ."

"Really? Well. She had a bad dream, probably."

"A bad dream," I repeat.

"I don't know. Yes. That's what she said." My grandmother shrugs this off with a stiff chuckle.

"Is she here? Did you talk to her?"

"I did."

"And did she seem okay this morning? Because she looked very distressed when—"

"*Yes.*"

I falter.

"It was a bad dream, I told you. That is what she told me," Eliza snaps, "nothing else. Okay?"

Instantly apologetic, she pats my shoulder. With a nod, I fold my lips shut. But I know she is lying. Shehani comes out with a watering can looking jumpy, her usually sleek hair ruffled, her eyes darting. She mumbles her 'hallo'. Atay, meanwhile, is as still and silent as ever; I can see her inside when I crane my neck, standing rigid over Rita.

I blink in the sunlight. There is a sound like seeping gas as Shehani tips her spout into the flower pots. My grandmother shifts from foot to foot.

Then my phone rings; an unknown number. Turning away, I breathe my relief into the microphone. "Hello?"

"Daniela?"

"Yes. Who is this?"

"Chris," the voice introduces itself. It is gruff and meandering, as if the man it belongs to is distracted from his own sentences, turning his head halfway through them. He is the manager of that coffee shop, Chest, where I applied for a job. "I want to interview you."

"Of course," I chatter, plunging a finger in my ear to stop the noise of the crickets. "Please, yes. Anytime."

"How about this morning? We're not very busy."

"Yes," I say again, too quickly, "I can come straight in."

Hanging up, I look at my phone for the first time since my rashly sent message to Paris last night, to which he replied, 'Yeah. Do you want to come over?'

I blush, stuff my phone into my bag. "I have to go," I tell my grandmother.

"You got an interview? Ah." Her felicitations are fleeting. "*Now*? Where? Good luck," she calls after me. "Let us know when you get out."

"I will," I say.

I hardly have time to wonder who the manager is before he strides towards me, his black T-shirt saying 'I'm Your Man' with a photo of Leonard Cohen for the 'I'.

"Daniela?"

"Yes. How did you know?"

"You look nervous." Chris smiles, his mouth soft amidst the patchy grey stubble on his chin. It matches that on his head, which I can see from the head of height that I have over him. "Have a seat."

"Thanks."

I do as he says. My eyes move of their own accord to the corner table where I sat alone, making eyes at Paris until he joined me outside. I can still sense him across the dimly lit room, staring past the pillows on assorted chairs, past the jungle of plants both potted and hanging, at me. But his table is empty.

"Tell me about yourself," Chris says, leaning back against a low green sofa. Peaches pattern its fabric. "What brings you here?"

A girl puts two glasses down on the table between us, along with two bottles of water. Their plastic protests when she lets them go.

I explain that I have come from England to be with my family and Chris asks whether I have a passport, the right to work here. I tell him I do. Perhaps things would be easier if I did not, I reflect, as he makes note and moves on to the next question; the fewer options you have, the fewer decisions need making. Where would I be now if I had been born an English girl, not just a girl in England?

"Okay. So, you're twenty-one. What have you been doing since you finished school? More studying? A degree?"

"No, no degree," I say, in what I hope is a pleasant enough tone, "I've just been working." I glance at the girl who brought us

121

our water and wonder when this statement lost its value, why I should have to preface it with the word 'just', sheepishly, when I am applying to work in a coffee shop.

"Ah, okay." Chris nods. "So you've had jobs like this before. That's good."

"Yes."

My CV sits, evidently unread, on the sofa beside him.

"And what do you want to do long term?" he asks.

At this, I look to a string of fairy lights on the stone wall, as if they might flash me the answer. "Erm . . ."

He gives another soft smile, waves a hand. "Don't worry. I know this isn't anyone's dream. It's a stopgap until you figure out what is, and that's fine. As long as you work hard for me in the meantime. Are you a good team player?"

"Yes," I say, struck by his directness. "Actually, I think I work better in a team."

"That's good. Everyone is very friendly. It will be nice for you, if you've just moved here."

I nod, grateful of his encouragement. Still, I cannot help but wonder where I might be if I didn't need it, if I weren't severed like this city is down the middle. Perhaps I would be back working at Oxfam, sharing tea and biscuits with the semi-retired ladies who were my colleagues. With them, I could speak philosophically but never about politics, could show them photos from my trips here, just not of my father and his beard in

England. Occasionally, a middle-aged man, smiling and determined on his quest to save the world, would come in from head office to see how we were doing. Mark, usually. He would stay for tea, too.

Across the coffee table, Chris raises his eyebrows at me. "Do you have any questions? About the team, or anything else?"

I consider this. It is a young team, I can see that, so it will be different to Oxfam, socially. I won't be able to ask after anyone's grandchildren. Perhaps, in a different way, I will like it just as much. But will I be just as restless, too? Thinking about the western side of myself, be it American or English, neither or both, that I have left behind. Will it distract me like this part of me did, despite my enjoyment of making charitable transactions, as it hammered and screamed at the insides of my head and chest? Drowning out Travis, making me blink over the till at the pale hands proffering rumpled shirts, at the pale faces on cocked heads when I didn't react straight away. Will this be better for me, more fitting? Will I feel that I have come to the right place, at last? Or is my mother right, and should I have gone to university after all? I feel more wary of this every time someone assumes that I did and I have to say otherwise. I feel lesser, like I should apply. But what would I study? Surely not knowing that is a poor start. Isn't it too late, anyway?

"No questions," I say. "I think you've told me everything I need to know."

Chris caps his pen. "Great. I'd like to get you in for your first shift, if you're happy."

I blink. "Yeah. Of course."

"When are you available?"

Once again I look to the fairy lights, glinting in the morning sun, then back at Chris. "Anytime," I say.

Nineteen

I can smell the charcoal burning from across the street where Maria parks and she, George and I climb out of her car, into the evening. A warm breeze carries the smoke towards us. We follow it to my grandparents' house, which has disappeared behind higher levels of security as they have aged; Eliza's anxieties have amplified.

"Welcome," she greets us, when we have made it past the front gate.

"Hallo, hallo," Andreas echoes.

His arms are flung wide, hers pinned behind her back, until I step closer and she folds me into a hug.

"How are you?"

"Good, good . . ."

There are kisses all around. At the touch of a remote control, a second gate opens and cameras swivel to catch us passing through it. Andreas closes it behind us, again with the press of a button. This technology feels too advanced for a road that fades to dust at the edges; the neighbourhood lacks pavements, despite its proximity to the city centre. My grandparents' house, as a result, with its flat roof of solar panels and the extra floor that drops down at the back, out of sight, gives the impression of a rural compound.

I catch my breath. "The garden looks amazing."

"Haven't you seen it yet?" my grandmother asks, her hooked nose pouring even further over itself as she frowns, "You must have."

"It wasn't like this though. All these flowers," I say, catching their delicate scents as I lean to tuck back my hair. "Everything's bloomed since the last time."

When was the last time? It can't have been more than two weeks ago and yet, just streets away, my grandparents' garden has erupted into plumes of roses, hydrangeas, chrysanthemums. The surrounding cactuses bristle. They are biding their time until winter, I imagine, when these petals will shrivel and fall, and the garden will be theirs once again. Round the back, the lemon trees keep to themselves.

"Please, sit," Andreas bids me.

What once was an ornate iron gate has been pressed, like another flower, between two sheets of glass and mounted on legs for a table. I take a seat at one end.

"Does anyone want a drink?" my grandmother asks. "We have beer, wine, juice . . ."

"Whiskey," my grandfather interjects, his face plastered with a grin.

"Whiskey," Eliza repeats, rolling her eyes, "if you want."

"I will have whiskey," George announces, from the opposite end of the table.

He and my grandfather descend into giddy laughter. Chuckling along, Eliza re-emerges from the kitchen with two tumblers and a glass of white wine for me. Maria follows, carrying a salad she has prepared inside. Next she brings out metal pokers studded with cubes of meat, which Andreas suspends over the fire in spinning rows. Their aroma draws saliva to my tongue and cats to the perimeter. With its nose in the air, one of them creeps along the wall to the dome of the built-in oven, where smoke is rising from a chimney. Eliza jumps to scare it off, as frantically as if it is a human intruder that has entered her fortress, not this hungry, wide-eyed creature.

"So," she addresses me, when we are sitting down to eat; the meat is dry and crusted with herbs, piled high on our plates and in a bowl mid-table. "How was your interview?"

"Oh, yeah." I gulp down a mouthful of bread with my wine. "I got the job."

"You got the job," she exclaims, her thick brows parting. "Excellent!"

"Bravo, Dani," Maria smiles.

Andreas does, too. As I describe my new role, everyone appears pleased except my great grandfather. I glance sideways at him, wary of how cynical he has been about my forsaking of London and its many opportunities, until my grandmother nudges him.

127

"Daniela, cheers," Andreas says. He beams, then knocks back his whiskey and gets up to replenish it. "Do you want another, George?"

My great grandfather waves a hand. "One is enough for me," he says, and burrows further down in his chair.

"You must tell your parents," Eliza prattles on in excitement, "I'll get the phone."

Potato turns to mush in my mouth. Before I can react, she is back outside, smiling into the receiver of her home phone, then thrusting it to my ear. My mother is on the line, asking how I am and saying well done. Is she proud of me? It is impossible to tell amidst the celebratory chatter and the clanging of cutlery against plates. Still, I doubt it. 'Waitress' hardly stacks up against the postgraduate jobs that her friends' children will be eligible for now. But have any of them moved abroad, secured work—any work—in a non-English-speaking country and integrated into its society? One or two may have 'found themselves' in a month of backpacking through Thailand, but that cannot be half as brave as getting lost in a place completely. Although, I think, as my mother's voice drones on in my ear, I have been speaking this language all my life. I didn't go out of my way to learn it. I have family here, friends. I am paying bills, but otherwise living rent-free in a small flat of my own. Defensiveness dissolves to horror in my throat. Is what I have achieved worth noting at all?

"We've booked to come out and see you, by the way."

"When?"

"In a few weeks' time," my mother says.

"Good," I hear myself say. "Great. That will be nice."

"No need to sound too excited," she scoffs. "What's the matter? Is something wrong?"

"Nothing's wrong, Mom." *Mom*. Her contribution to my incongruent upbringing. "I'm fine. Looking forward to it."

When we hang up, I feel disorientated. Everyone has stopped talking and laughing to look at me, expectantly. I am overwhelmed with the sense that my life is on display—my parents will scrutinise it, when they arrive—and I am still not sure it is ready, not sure how presentable my choices have made it. I pass the phone back to my grandmother, jaw clenched. I want to snap at her for springing it on me, but I know she must ache to call her own mother with good news, bad news, no news at all; she would give anything for what I have got.

Putting on a smile, I say, "Well, I guess I had better start cleaning."

"Cleaning?" Eliza shakes her head. "Why?"

"You know Mom. Very hygiene conscious."

"Ah, yes. That's true." Her laughter recedes into the creases around her eyes. "You know, if you ever need help, Shehani can come upstairs."

129

"Really," I respond, picking up my knife and fork. This is a kind offer, but I hardly need the assistance. I haven't earned it, I think darkly, and grip the butt of my knife hard enough that it hurts.

"Of course," my grandmother says. Oblivious, she shovels in another mouthful of pork. "You just have to ask her."

Twenty

I have agreed to meet Paris outside H&M, in the pedestrianised part of the city. He is standing there in ripped black jeans and a T-shirt when I arrive, his necklace glinting in the sun, his red trainers as bold as new.

"Hi," I start, before he thrusts a branded bag at me like a dummy.

It is effective, for a moment, while I peer inside. Between its handles, above the hot cobbles and below the blue sky, lies a tangle of lace. I flinch from it, mortified. The bag responds with a rustle. No one has ever gifted me something so daring as lingerie.

A memory arises, of Beyza and I sloping off from a party while we were sleeping together, unbeknownst to our friends. We started slowly that night, stirring one another up while still fully clothed. Her underwear was warm when I pulled it off. Mine was, too. When we were finished, she snatched it away from me and put it on herself, eyes shining.

"And you wear mine," she said.

We scurried back downstairs tittering, my head so hot with lust I could hardly see straight, and played out the rest of the party like nothing had happened. Only we knew.

Behind his sunglasses, Paris smiles. They are so dark I cannot see his eyes, and yet I feel that he is watching me, closely.

I shake myself, let the bag fall to my side. "Thanks, but . . . You kind of disappeared. Again."

Has this bothered him? It is impossible to tell, yet my lenses are as transparent as his are impassive. He must know what I am referring to: our exchange the night before my interview, after my encounter with Beyza, when I texted to ask if he was awake and he replied inviting me over. The following evening, I sent back an earnest paragraph of explanation, saying I was in a strange headspace and that it had caught me off guard to meet someone I liked so much. I didn't hear back until this morning, when he sent one line asking me to meet him here. It has been days.

Somehow, Paris shifts closer without moving a muscle. "I'm here now, aren't I? Come on," he says, his lips curving up at the corners, "I'll make it up to you."

He leads the way down a side street and into the reception area of a darkened building. Dust clings to the frames of black-and-white photographs on the walls, and there is no one behind the front desk. I receive no answer when I ask if we are allowed inside.

"How do you feel about lifts?"

"I don't know," I say, eyeing the worn arrowed buttons, the paint scuffed and peeling around the metal doors. "I think I'd prefer to take the stairs."

"Okay," Paris responds, in a warning tone. When we have scaled five flights, he grins over his shoulder. "How about now?"

I groan, only partly in jest.

"We're almost halfway."

On the eleventh floor, we come to a one-room museum with panoramic views over the city. Paris pays two-fifty for each of us to get in—he insists—and there is no one else, just us and the woman behind the till. Her wrinkled hands, the bulbous moles on her neck.

Behind a curtain in the centre, a video crackles on a loop; footage from the conflict. I am transfixed by the men in jeans poking guns around street corners, by the fact that this happened here, just ten storeys below me, and so recently. Along the artificially cooled wall, I trace a timeline of our civilization from occupation to occupation. Like this island was an empty stall, I think, disgusted, with one drunken power bursting in after another. Even now we are not alone. Not at war, perhaps, but we have never been left in peace.

I walk over to Paris at the window facing The North, where we can see our city as if it is still undivided.

"Welcome."

"Thanks."

"Beautiful, isn't it?" he says.

"Yes."

"And hideous."

133

I look at him. Only now has he removed his sunglasses. He is holding them in his fist, the knotted scar beneath his eyebrow glistening tight.

"That *was* a cathedral. The oldest surviving Gothic church in the country, it says here." He points at a note on the map before us.

"That's impressive."

"It's not though, is it? *Surviving*. They destroyed it. Look."

Following a more forceful jab of his finger down, I gasp to see the minarets thrust to piercing through its roof like spears.

"It was converted?" I'd had no idea this could be done to a church. "When?"

"In their last siege, or the one before that. Not that it matters." Paris shakes his head. "I have never cared about anything the way I care about this place. Or hated anything the way I hate that fucking flag," he spits.

I follow his hardened gaze back to the view, to our latest occupants' flag on the mountainside over the city. I am surprised to find that it looks smaller from here than it does from my kitchen, even though my flat is further away. We are higher up here, I suppose. And then I realise that as much as I am nodding along, agreeing with Paris, I am not glaring at it with half as much hatred as I usually would. The breath jerks from my lungs. Above the honking of cars and the cries of cats, above the crumbling pillars, the stacked balconies, the flat roofs and the oblong water tanks atop them, the flag does not provoke me as it means to. Never mind the seam—hidden, from up here—where the domes of our churches meet the turrets of theirs. It is Beyza. I am thinking of Beyza and wanting back Beyza and when I look at that flag now, I can't help but see Beyza, the place where she is. And yet I detest it. I *should* detest it, like Paris does; there is nothing torn or uncertain in the anger on his face. Until he turns it upon me.

Softening, he says, "I'm glad you're here, Daniela. We need people like you." As if I am an outsider, a British colonialist or an American soldier sent to 'save' the island after the discovery of some oil. I blink, hurt, before he affects a swoon and says, "Those *eyes*," rolling his. "I live over there, by the way."

"That's where my grandparents live," I start, following him back to the east-facing window. I point to a neighbourhood beyond the glass towers.

"Oh, really?"

"Yeah."

"So we're neighbours."

"Yeah," I repeat, half whispering this time. I gaze up at him, hope that he sees. We *are* neighbours.

A lock of hair falls over his temple. The assertive motion with which he brushes it back bolsters me, and I tip my chin up. He tilts his down to kiss me with his hands on my back. Slides them lower. I break away from him, blushing.

135

"Will I hear from you this time?" I ask him, when we are back outside H&M.

The cobbles are hotter under our feet, our knees weakened by the long descent.

Paris smirks. "You might just."

Twenty-One

'Hey, is this still your number?' Beyza texts me.

I blink. It is jarring to see her name light up my phone after so many years, like things are just as they were between us, and yet everything is different.

Lowering the thistle of mascara from my face, I reply, 'Yeah, this is me'.

On-screen, the words look too small and dull to have taken the amount of thought that they did. I cannot settle while I wait for her reply, cannot even finish coating my eyelashes without glancing down at the edge of the bathroom sink, where my phone is balanced. Swearing under my breath, I lean into the mirror and dab at them with a forefinger. It is no use. Try as I might to encourage them apart, they end up sticking back together.

Another chime sounds and I jump to see what Beyza has said.

'Cool . . . Could never quite manage to delete it haha'.

My stomach pulses. Tentatively, I let my thumbs explore the keyboard, press send. She does the same several times, then asks if I am free today.

'No,' I reply, in a rush of remorse, 'sorry. I have my first shift at a new job'.

'Okay. Good luck', comes her response, moments later.

In the harsh overhead light, I begin to fret she is hurt, that she thinks I don't want to see her and am making excuses. My fingernails slot in between my teeth.

Then: 'Let me know if you're around some other time'.

Exhaling, I lower them. After my date with Paris, there was a flurry in my stomach. I feel one like it now, only high in my chest and scattered by my heavy-beating heart.

'I will', I promise.

I watch for a message back and feel my shoulders slump when none comes, then adjust my stance in the mirror. It is time for work.

"Daniela. Good to see you again," Chris says, when I arrive.

He is wearing the same T-shirt he wore for my interview, and for the first time, I notice that the poet upon it is also accounted for in a photo on the wall. It is not signed, just framed. Around it hang similarly random shots of Joni Mitchell and Jimi Hendrix, amongst other musicians. Their lack of coordination to the surrounding space makes them, ironically, a perfect fit for it.

"Hi, Chris. How are you?"

He nods. "Well. Let me introduce you to your colleagues. Stephanie, Ivan, Anna . . ." He waves towards them each in turn. "This is Daniela."

"Hallo," they chorus.

The loudest voice belongs to Stephanie, who has her hair stretched back into swooping curls over her shoulders and wears a startling amount of makeup. Through it, she smiles tightly. Ivan appears to be the oldest of us, with indiscriminate tattoos loosely clinging to his biceps. I recognise the way in which he mumbles his greeting, as if ashamed he is here, that he has not yet moved beyond hospitality. Finally, I look to Anna. Her hair is as black as Stephanie's only cropped to her jaw, which is round beside the straight edge of her bob. Soft.

"There are others of course, but this is us for today," Chris concludes our meeting.

I blink the image of this short, sweet-looking girl with no makeup on from my eyes. Her keen though somewhat anxious face, her scent like powdered milk. She is pretty. So is Stephanie in a starker, skinnier way. Even Ivan has his features, strong hands and tepid eyes—he is Russian, I learn—features that could be seen as a threat, by Beyza.

I am relieved to get to work, though I don't know exactly what I am doing. Avoiding eye contact with my colleagues, mostly. With every question I ask them, every customer whose eyes linger upon me after they have been served, I think again of my sixth form experience and how it was marred for me. I find myself shying away from Anna in particular, just as I shied from those I deemed remotely attractive then, for fear of Beyza's wrath. By lunchtime I am asking myself, was this worth it? Could it ever be?

"Nice meeting you," Anna says, at the end of the day.

The sign above us barks 'Chest' like a command.

"You too," I smile.

Glance her off my body like a ball. Repel, deflect. I walk the wrong way out just to avoid her.

The sun is setting over the city, sending an orange glow into my bedroom. It reflects off the air conditioning unit that hangs above my bed and creates a sheen on the adjacent mirror. I wind the shutters down and step back from them into darkness. Now there is only one effervescent thing in this room, that which I have not been able to look at since I brought it in. The H&M bag. I walk over to it quietly, as if it might hear me coming and startle. Quite the opposite. The lace inside is soft to the touch. It unfurls like a shadow in my unlit bedroom. I hold it to me. Then, letting my thicker clothes slide to the floor, I pull on the new set. It clasps my back.

My hands float to my sides. In the dim light creeping from down the corridor, I can see: it fits me perfectly. How did Paris manage it? He has never seen me undressed, and the clothes I wear out are not all that close-fitting. He is practised, I think, he has gauged all sorts of girls' sizes. But this does not bother me as perhaps it should. Instead I feel seen. I am someone who can be looked over and determined with a number and a capital letter, I think. Paris has determined me, without deliberation or error. He has established my exact quantity, as I have been trying to do for years. I turn this way and that in the mirror, seeing myself both exactly as I am and as I could be, too. As he could make me.

My phone chimes with a text. Inexplicably guilty, I strip naked of the underwear, stash it in with my laundry and go to see who it is from.

Twenty-Two

Shehani is manoeuvring my great aunt out of her armchair when I enter their flat, with one of Rita's arms splayed over her shoulders. Atay constricts the other.

"Oh. Hi," I stammer. "Sorry."

Startled, Shehani manages a greeting through her gritted teeth. Atay does not say a word, nor does she look surprised to see me. Rita looks mesmerised, her fuzzy head cocked to one side, her eyes searching. They don't appear to find anything.

I clear my throat. "I can come back, if it's not a good time . . ."

"One moment."

With a final effort, Shehani hefts Rita up and onto her wheelchair. There is a flash of pale muscle, the only sign of cooperation between she and her co-worker before they both stand back.

Shehani smooths her hair. "Are you okay?"

"Yeah," I say, over the whirring of several fans. "How are you?"

She responds with a gesture that is half a smile, half a shrug. "Are you looking for someone? Your grandmother just left."

"Actually . . ." At the sight of the sweat on her forehead, I falter. "I've fallen behind with a few things since I started my new job. Do you think . . ? Well. I was going to ask you, but . . ."

Shehani shakes her head, a strained look upon her face; my blather has been chopped to bits by the many blades in motion. She steps closer. I shouldn't have listened to my grandmother. I shouldn't have come here seeking help just because I could, I realise, backing away. Shehani works hard for Eliza, just as Eliza worked hard for someone else throughout her career; this is the condition upon which their relationship stands. What have I done to contribute?

"Sorry, I didn't hear you." Shehani takes another step towards me.

Fearing her touch, her tragic conviction that she will be able to connect with her daughter through me, I blurt out, "Could you help me clean my flat?"

"Of course," she says, no questions asked. She ceases her advance.

I feel relieved, then guilty for it. "If you have time, I mean. If not, I'll manage."

"I have time," she says, just as quickly.

I look at her.

"We are not *both* needed here."

This comment is pointed. It injects a cooler air than the fans do into the room, to another flinch of Atay's slender bicep. Otherwise, she only stares after Shehani and I as we step out into the sun. My skin prickles. We walk around the building and up the stairs to my flat.

"So, how is work?" Shehani asks, brighter now that we are alone. "You are busy?"

"Yes," I say.

I don't meet her eyes. Work has not kept me so busy that I couldn't find time to sweep, or bleach the toilet, or wipe grape vinegar up the kitchen wall to deter ants. In truth, I have invited Paris to spend the evening here—he texted me after our date, which must mean he is more committed than he was—and I want to make a good impression. Of course, I also want to keep this quiet; I can't imagine it would please my grandparents to see a man of almost thirty emerge from my door tomorrow morning. I turn my key in the lock. I set the fans in motion on every ceiling, large wooden wheels to steer the ship of my flat through summer's heat waves.

Then I ask, "How about you?"

"Me?"

"How is your work, at the moment? With Atay."

Shehani scratches her head but does not break eye contact. Or blink. "My work is fine."

Fine, I echo, internally. It appears we are both withholding something. Fine. "Let's start in the bathroom, maybe. Do you want a glass of water or anything?"

Shehani says she is okay for the moment and we get to work, her with her hand plunged wrist-deep down the shower drain, me with my nose wrinkled at the stench, scrubbing the toilet seat. As we dust and polish, take things off shelves and put them back again, I notice that she is still scratching her head. Earlier, I thought it was a sign of discomfort, that she didn't want to answer my questions. Evidently her itching is endless. I curse myself for neglecting to put any music on, for now I have to listen to the sound of her nails against her scalp like tiny saws at work, spraying dust. The thought of lice enters my head. I recoil from the flakes of dandruff that fall to my freshly cleaned sink as Shehani leans over to wash her hands. Her black hair is as full of it as if she has gone out in the snow, only it is forty degrees outside.

She straightens, breathless, to scratch again.

"Are you okay?" I ask, removing my body wash from the shower in preparation to wipe down its shelf. "Your head . . ."

"Yes, I am okay," she says, "Just itchy. I never had this problem before." She gestures, helpless, her rubber gloves like yellow warning signs.

Another bottle from the shelf weighs heavily in my hands. "Maybe you should try a new shampoo," I suggest, lamely.

Shehani gives a faint smile. "Maybe," she replies.

It is with a tight smile that I open the door. Even though I like Paris, I invited him here, I am looking at him without seeing him. Then I am bowing my head.

I shut the door behind him with a 'click' and the silence engulfs us. For the second time today I wish I had left the radio on or a window open or something, anything that might have made this space seem less expectant. Stale, contrived. Paris has sprayed nothing but deodorant on himself, and a tang of his sweat has just started to break through.

"How are you?" he asks.

"Not bad." My face feels thin behind my high-arched brows. That part of my brain is taking over again, the part that always does this close to sex with someone new. A pretence of coolness comes over me from some terrified childish place, like when you trip and fall in a crowded playground and have to walk calmly over to your parents, biting your tears back and saying you're fine when you are screaming inside, in agony. It is sexier not to get caught up in it, or not to let on if you do. I have been told this with absolute certainty. There are lots of things I would like to hear from Paris, lots of things I would like to say to him, but now is not the time. "How are you?" is as far as I push it.

"Better now." Bright-eyed, he steps towards me.

And then I cease to see him again, his black shorts, his white shirt and the silver chain beneath its collar. Instead I see Oscar, the first boy ever to touch me. I was still reeling from my breakup with Beyza, in sixth form. One of the new students had started telling people he liked me, and I, as ever, was uncertain of my feelings on the matter. So I slept with him. He had brown hair

146

and bruised skin, was very tall and quick to finish. Afterwards I told a female classmate that I was puzzled because I had not felt much except some mild discomfort. No pleasure. The whole experience had been awkward and underwhelming, for me. My classmate assured me that it was often like that the first time, for girls at least. I just needed to try again with someone else and I would enjoy it more then.

When the opportunity presented itself, I took her advice. Samuel was the other boy's name. He looked washed out next to Oscar, with paper skin, grey eyes and hair that should have been blonde but somehow seemed colourless. Like the beach on an overcast day. I thought I might make something of it, of him. We ended up back in his single bed after a handful of dates, and still I felt almost nothing. It was clumsy, teenaged fumbling.

I blink and there is Paris again, a breath away from me, that white knot beneath his eyebrow pulling taut around my knees.

"Aren't you going to offer me a drink?" he asks, with a smirk.

"Oh . . ." The apologies cascade from my mouth, reddening my cheeks on their way out. Yes, I am definitely still attracted to boys, in spite of it all, which has confused me for years. "What do you drink? Beer, wine? Or something else?"

"I'll have a beer. Thanks."

It flashes through my mind as I am pouring him one that I am glad I went out, after Shehani left, and bought this selection of lager, red wine, white wine, not knowing what Paris might want. I

147

am glad that I bothered cleaning, too. I did consider not doing it in case I lost my nerve and backed out, or he let me down again.

And again he is there when I turn around. I jolt, almost dropping his drink. "Here you go."

Without taking his eyes off me, Paris takes the glass in one hand and the bottle in the other, parting its yellow label with his fingers.

My hands go limp at my sides. "Have you been working?"

"Yeah," he says. "I haven't been the best at texting back, I know. Big week."

"That's okay," I assure him, as if he has apologised properly. As if I have any idea what a 'big week' in security entails or why he should have to. I am blushing, mumbling, "Down payments don't earn themselves, I guess."

At this, Paris raises his eyebrows. "No," he muses, moving his eyes over the room and then back to me. "Parents earn them. Right?"

My laughter sticks in my throat. I open my mouth to explain that this is temporary, I didn't ask for it and don't believe I should be entitled to it at all—quite the opposite—but no sound comes out. Paris returns his beer to the countertop, pushes my back to it and kisses me. I kiss him back in my same preoccupied way, thinking about what this is leading to, what it will be like and whether we will get away with it without my family catching him on his way out—*if* they didn't spy him coming in. I should pull him closer, I think, perhaps let out a sigh.

Then the world lurches downwards; Paris throws me up by my waist and catches me at his. I gasp into his mouth and he pushes warm breath back at mine. I seem to weigh so much less in his eyes and in his arms. I kiss him harder, forgetting inhibition, forgetting everything as my surroundings shift again, this time sideways into my bedroom.

I land with another gasp on my back, on my mattress that is covered by white sheets and no duvet, and even then is too hot to lie still on. Paris turns on the fan. There is a rush of air as he leans over, pulls off my clothes to reveal the underwear he bought for me and murmurs approvingly. He disappears from my view.

I watch the fan gathering speed, breath held, until he touches between my legs. It spins faster, I moan and then he is inside me. No thinking now, no putting anything on for his benefit. I am lost in the spinning of the fan round and round, the driving of his body into mine forwards and back. It speeds up, all of it, so I am breathless trying to keep up, arching to fill my lungs until, with a final thrust, Paris stops.

The fan keeps spinning, dizzying. I let my head fall back onto the bed. He slips out of the room to clean himself up. I close my eyes and listen to the post-coital bathroom sounds of toilet paper tearing, the bin clanging open and closed, water running down the drain. My breath evens out. Relief spreads through my body as I relax into the mattress; all this time I have worried something might be wrong with me, but Paris has shown me that it is not. He has made me feel that all is right. *I* am right, with him.

I am still lying naked on my back when he returns. He pauses in the doorway, and in the half-darkness I see him move a hand in and out from his pelvis, experimentally. Giddy laughter rises in my throat. He wants me again. Even when he gives up on his too-recently spent body, this knowledge delights me. For the first time he lies down beside me and I turn towards him. The smell of his sweat is stronger now, and even more sordidly appealing to me than it was when he arrived.

"Are you okay?" he asks. There is no trace of obligation to his tone. Some smugness perhaps, but only as much as mutual satisfaction assures.

I scoff. "*Yes*. Are you?"

"No."

I laugh, which seems to please him. He strokes his fingers down my arm.

"Where did you get that scar?"

"The army," he says, after a moment. His hand has fallen still.

"What division were you?"

No answer.

"My father was in the infantry," I say, to fill the silence. To prove once again that I am not an outsider in this place, pouring over its plight like some twisted pornography. If ever Jason moves back here, he will be given a gun and made to report to annual training. He will become a reserve, whether he likes it or not, as every able-bodied man here has to. "Paris?" I probe.

"Engineers Command," he says at last, his voice hoarse. "De-mining." Nothing more.

For a moment I fear he will roll away from me, that I have pushed him too far, as far as the door, he will slam it behind him and never look back. But he does not. He simply sweeps back a strand of his long hair, as if he might sweep the sheen of whitened skin away with it. Very shiny for something dead, that bit of skin, I think, it could be the most vital part of him. And yet it is unspoken.

Paris remains attentive all night, and sneaks out of my flat undetected in the morning. Perhaps we have turned a corner, I think. But he doesn't respond to my texts the next day.

Twenty-Three

On my way out to work two days later, I see Shehani tending to the bougainvillaea outside Rita's flat. Fuchsia-pink bracts plume around her head like epiphanies. There is nothing unusual about this, of course, except that it is the first time I have seen her since she helped me clean my flat.

"Good morning." I stop at the gate, intending to thank her.

She turns her watering can upright so there is no more trickling from its spout, just the static hum of invisible crickets. Her eyes look wet.

"Hallo," she murmurs.

Once again, I wonder if she is looking at me and seeing her daughter, just as I looked at Paris and saw the faces of the boys I had been involved with before, briefly. By the end of our night together, it was only us. And what has become of him since?

Shaking my face from the grip of a blush, I peer closer at Shehani. Perhaps she is not crying tears of emotion after all. Her pupils are small, their surrounding whites bloodshot; she is sniffling like she is full of cold in forty degrees, and there are still those flakes of dandruff in her hair.

"Is everything okay?" I ask, swallowing yet another urge to back away from her. "You don't look well."

"I'm fine," she tells me. But she has to clear her throat twice before explaining that she did not sleep well last night, and so is feeling a bit rundown. "Rita is getting worse. She wakes up all night needing the toilet now, so we have to take her in and out. If we don't hear her call, she wets the bed. I changed the sheets twice last night."

I fight the grimace that tugs at my mouth as Shehani does her temple. My poor great aunt seems to get constantly sicker, yet no closer to the death she desires. I cannot think of anything worse than so vibrant a life ending in a dreary hospice dorm, as hers inevitably will. So I don't.

"You should talk to Atay. Maybe she'll take over this afternoon so you can get some rest. You look like you need it."

At this suggestion, Shehani turns over her shoulder with eyes that go wide at the rims, while her pupils remain pinched. "Yes," she says, unconvincingly.

I don't know what I expected, advising her to ask a favour from someone she would not choose to confide in, for one reason or another. She is visibly reluctant. I am less so, hitching the strap of my bag higher up my shoulder and waving goodbye to her; the problem is someone else's now. Perhaps I am wrong to flee from it, but I wouldn't know how to help. I imagine I would just stand there, scuffing my shoes, feeling sorry for having been born into my life and not one like hers; not to mention that I have added to her workload this week, for the sake of one frivolous night. Where *is* Paris? I banish this thought with a shake of my head. Apart from the guilt, I have my own job. I can't be late in my first week.

The absoluteness of this reassures me as I approach my aunt's car. Since it is too hot now to walk into town, we have agreed to start carpooling; our hours will be similar until I am trained for evening shifts. She has her seatbelt on ready to go when I climb in beside her, with the air conditioning blasting, pop music playing on the radio.

"Hallo," she says, her voice as hoarse as Shehani's.

Alarmed, I look at her. It relieves me to see that the whites of her eyes are just that: white. Her hair is tousled and matted, but not flecked with dry scalp. I let my head rest against the seat. Maria is well. She is simply not a morning person. She parks by the square that edges the older end of the city and we go our separate ways.

Outside Chest, I take out my phone. I will need to switch it off for the day, but not before pausing over the message I sent to Paris after our night together, the message he still hasn't replied to.

'Thanks for last night . . . lucky no one caught us . . . can't stop thinking about you . . . can I call you when I get–'

Off.

Stuffing the device back into my pocket, I look down the street at the crossing point to the Other Side, to Beyza. I waver. Then I step inside.

Twenty-Four

Several trips to and from town later, Paris texts me. I am back in my aunt's car, heading in for another shift of scribbling orders, polishing glasses, serving drinks; iced coffees, iced waters, rose cordials. The car inches forwards in traffic. Am I free today, Paris has asked me.

"Dani."

"Sorry?"

"Bubblegum." Maria shakes a packet at me, not taking her eyes off the road. "Do you want some?"

"Oh. Yes please."

I don't think I do, really, but something compels me to slide a stick of it out, onto my tongue. Perhaps it is the smell of it filling her car. It has pervaded since I can remember, this smell, of pink. Not strawberry or raspberry or any flavour, particularly. Just pink, I thought as a child. It pools between my teeth.

Looking again at Paris's message, I feel my forehead crease. I am baffled that he would ask to see me by text, after ignoring the last one I sent him. It must be there, a bubble above this proposition on his phone as it is upon mine, and he hasn't even acknowledged it. Why not message straight back if he likes me? Why bother at all if he does not? A motorcyclist weaves around our car to the front of the queue and I glare at the food delivery box at his back. I consider leaving Paris without a response for twenty-four hours, seeing how he likes it. Then the light turns green and the motorcyclist is gone. Maria accelerates after him.

Perhaps I should take a leaf from my grandmother's book. With a sideways glance, I reflect on the efforts she has made to conceal Maria's practices from me, just as the horrors of Katerina's disappearance were secreted from her. With all her fussing and hushing, Eliza gives herself the illusion of control, even if she does not affect change. I could try doing the same thing, I think; granting myself *some* reassurance by denying Paris any, just for a while.

As we near the city centre, I return to a text I received earlier, from Beyza.

'How are you doing?' it says.

My heart fumbles for the words to write back.

"Do you finish at six tonight?" my aunt asks, oblivious.

"Yes. Erm? Yeah. I think so."

"Me too. Maybe we can go somewhere to eat, before we go home?"

"Sure," I say, without looking up from my phone.

I check it once more before I go into work.

'Free this afternoon? Let's have coffee. We can go back to my place after', Paris has said in a second text, and signed off with a wink-face.

His place. I hesitate. This has an enticing ring of ownership to it, an assurance I lack despite living alone; without an official rental agreement, my situation is comparatively flimsy. There is also the fact that I am not paying for it, which I am sure he respects even less than I do. The smell of coffee stirs me and I wish I had heard from him days ago. I like Paris, but he is so unreliable. I can never be sure where I stand with him, or whether he will catch me if I fail to.

Rounding off my exchange with Beyza, who has come back to me instantly, I enter Chest. A treasury. I will have to use every resource I have sealed in mine.

Ten to six. The light is fading as the sun sinks lower in the sky. I imagine it leaning in to disclose a secret. Soon the earth will shiver in response, the lamps in this coffee shop will be switched to glowing as its function shifts to bar, and I will be going home. Glancing again at the time in the bottom corner of the till screen, I feel my shoulders slump. The soles of my feet ache from standing. My knuckles are raw with rubbing the spill-stains off of tables, my middle and index fingers cramped from taking orders with a tiny pencil, and there are still eight minutes to go. Eight minutes, I try to buoy myself. That is nothing after nine hours.

"Daniela," Chris's voice sounds.

In an attempt to appear less spent, I smile as he approaches. "Yes?"

"There's a couple outside, on Bucket Table. They haven't ordered anything for an hour," he says, tapping his watch, "and I want free seats for my drinkers. Will you check on them for me?"

"Check on them," I repeat.

"Ask if they want anything else," he instructs me, then shrugs, "If they say no, just bring them the bill."

I eye the cluster of shot glasses between us, each one buffed and ready to roll a receipt up inside. "Okay," I say.

Chris takes my place at the till as I walk away, straightening up to appear taller behind it. I have not yet seen the people he speaks of. This place is split up into so many higgledy sections and hidden away corners that I often do not see people at all. For the last hour, I have been tied up with customers inside. Not only is 'Bucket Table' out front, it is also tucked behind a hulking green pail and obscured by the leaves of the olive tree inside. I have to wait for a gap in the stream of passers-by to walk around it, to tend to this one lonesome table. I wouldn't think to do so without knowing for a fact that someone was sitting there. A couple, according to Chris.

The girl is fine-featured, I notice at once, with slight shoulders and slender arms. Her manicured fingernails are held up for display by the man opposite her, who is running his thumbs in arcs over the backs of her hands. They must feel lovely to touch, I

159

think, soft with care. Then I feel stupid for thinking it. This is the kind of girl that makes me shrink into myself, the kind of girl I wish I was but am not even worthy of admiring.

"Can I get anything else for you?" I ask, rounding the table with my head bowed.

Cigarette smoke curls from it, sweet with the girl's fragrance. She is giggling at something her date must have said, something bold with suggestion, I infer from her biting her lip, eyes shining as she looks at him. Then I look at him. My first thought is that this man has his long hair tied back in a bun like Paris's, the tendrils peeking out at the nape of his neck like those I twirled between my fingertips, his neck itself a replica of the one I kissed and made clammy with my ragged breath, just nights ago. I imagine laying my head in its curve. There is a stab at my heart and I realise, I have. I did. Just nights ago.

No. I shake my head. He stares back at me with wide eyes until the scar above one of them twitches and I cannot deny; it is Paris, holding the hands of this other girl. I stumble back a step as she looks from him to me, me to him and back again, her oval face folding into a neat frown. For a moment I think he has brought her on purpose, to punish me for ignoring his texts. But I am sure I have never told him that I work here, not specifically. He has never asked. The shock on his face is genuine; he thought he would get away with this, as he does with everything. Can I get anything else for them, I have asked. Humiliation breaks out in red rashes across my cheeks. Still no one answers me.

"Or maybe you've had enough," I say, quietly.

And I retreat from the table, my vision blurred with tears. Mercifully, my shift is over.

Twenty-Five

"Dani," my aunt greets me.

She seems alarmed by the smile I shoot at her, and I realise I must look as stiff with fury as I feel, forcing it. We have met at a restaurant where green Carlsberg umbrellas stick up from tables spilling across the square. To one side of them, pedestrians and the cobbled street from which I have come. To the other, honking cars and the glass high-rises of the last decade.

"Do you want to sit out here or inside?"

"I don't know, wherever. You choose," I say, distracted.

There is no sign of Paris over my shoulder. Good, I think, I don't want to see him. And yet I cannot stop looking.

"Well, we have to order our food inside anyway."

"Right. Okay."

There is a rush of air conditioning inside the glass doors, cooling the monochrome floor.

The man behind the counter nods at us. "What can I get for you?"

At this, my anger frays. Shame begins to creep in at its edges and I fight to stop it, to stop seeing the look on Paris's face when I asked this same question and he had no answer, just moments ago, with that beautiful girl sitting opposite him.

"Chicken, please," my aunt says.

162

I scan the menu propped up by her elbow. Pita bread, salad, chips and dips all come with a portion of meat, or with the salty cheese produced exclusively on this island.

"Pork," I say.

I need something red-blooded. Red wine. Here, a glass costs the equivalent of one pound. It tastes at once metallic and sweet, like someone has bled into high-concentrate juice. I gulp it back with a grimace.

"You seem upset," Maria says.

An older woman has followed us back outside to a rickety wooden table, which winces at the tray of cutlery and condiments she puts down on it.

"Thanks," I say to her, and to my aunt, "I'm fine."

"Are you?"

"*Yes.*" It is all I can do not to hiss at her.

Our waitress waddles away. Around us, children squeal—we are early, for dinner—while cats slink up to the legs of their chairs and stare. Some get lucky with solicitously tossed scraps. Most do not. There is a clatter at the next table; the waitress has spilled some water. While she sighs and bustles inside to fetch a cloth, one of these less fortunate creatures gulps down the droplets, craning its neck and hanging its mouth open to catch them as they fall from the edge of the table. Then, with a sweep of the woman's cloth, the cat is cut off. It looks up with large green eyes and mewls after her as she walks away again, its throat hoarse. The heat presses in on me with a new persistence.

My aunt cocks her head. Am I upset, she wants to know. I have told her, I'm fine.

"Are you sure?" she asks, gently.

I bow my eyes into my fists. "Do you remember that guy who stood me up? We were supposed to go on a date . . ."

"Yes," Maria says, "I remember."

"Well, I didn't tell anyone but I saw him again. I slept with him, and . . ." In spite of my scrunched eyes, the tears rise in my throat. "He went out with another girl today, I saw him. Just because I didn't reply to his text. *One* text."

People are looking. I sense their attentions wandering from their own conversations to ours and sit upright.

"Sorry," I sniff.

Maria takes my hand across the table. "He shouldn't treat you like this. He shouldn't," she repeats firmly, despite the disappointment in her eyes. "This is not the way . . ."

I look at her.

"We cannot control other people's actions, only our own. Unfortunately," she adds, though the dismay has drained from her face; in an instant, she has calmed. "We can choose how we react to things. Loss, hurt. All these things."

"Chicken?"

I look up. The waitress has returned, this time bearing our food. Maria lets go of my hand to raise hers in the air, and I become aware of the sweat that has formed between our palms. The chicken is placed before her, the pork before me.

"Anything else?"

She catches my eye. "More wine?"

"Please," I say to the waitress, too keenly.

We do not resume speaking until she has gone and come back with the drink. I raise it to my lips, the smell of warm salt and herbs rising from my plate.

Maria nudges a cube of meat around hers. "I told you, when the time came for me to give up on art, faith was my truest comfort."

In vain, I cast around for the green-eyed cat. My aunt is watching me, evenly, when I look back at her.

"You didn't come to that service in the end," she says.

I chew and swallow a mouthful of pita bread. "No."

"You didn't want to?"

"It's not that. I just . . ." The Sunday she is referring to flashes through my mind, from the speeding taxi, to my crossing the border, to my meeting with Beyza beyond. "I got caught up. And it seems . . . I don't know. Our family . . ."

"They have their opinions," Maria says, her tone turned harsher again. She waves a hand.

165

Once again I am left feeling that there is something I don't know. The uncertainty of it, of everything, overwhelms me in a clattering drop of cutlery to my plate. More people look and I let them.

"Dani . . ."

"Do you still paint, Aunty?" I ask, imploringly, "ever?"

A boy streaks past on a skateboard, scattering pedestrians. Maria gives a sad smile. Above it, her brown eyes appear to be wilting. They are veiled in the nude sparkle they always are, reminding me of the My Little Ponies whose long hair she used to plait with me.

"You can come and look at my old paintings anytime," she says, as fresh tears start to slip down my cheeks.

I don't bother wiping them this time, nor do I bow my head to hide them. What's the point? It seems so futile, the meaning I have been searching for in life, when in reality it is callous and accidental and will move blindly on without the things I love if I fail to hold them close enough.

"Whatever happens," my aunt persists, "just remember there is someone with you, who will fortify you."

God, I think as the green-eyed cat sidles up to our table and I tip an offering of water and meat onto the ground. Maria is talking about her god again, Jehovah, yet in her words I find another meaning.

"They are making all things new. They will wipe out every tear from your eyes and the pain will be no more. These words are faithful and true. Draw close to them, and they will draw close to you . . ."

I don't get in the car and go home after our meal, as she does. Instead, I do as she *says*. Walk back into the pedestrianised part of the city. Past work. Past the table where Paris sat with that other girl behind the olive tree, behind my back. Keep walking with it turned to The South.

The North

Twenty-Six

"No."

"It's true."

"I don't believe it. *Her*?"

"Yep," Beyza grins.

A warm wind ruffles her hijab. We are sitting with the backs of our chairs turned in towards another coffee shop, around the corner from the one with the swings. Canvases dapple the paved garden behind us, painted with 'doors of the old city'. Most of these are ornate iron, emulous green or weathered to rotting. Some are uninhabited and sealed with padlocks, I noticed when passing through to the toilet—and on our walk here, in real life— though the windows above their locks were smashed in. Even this contradiction, this futility, is portrayed as lyrical here, in this one of several art cafes in the immediate area alone. I can't think of any on my side of the city. I wonder if their presence is what draws my aunt across the border.

Then I catch Beyza's eye and return to wondering about her teeth. She keeps her lips sealed when she smiles, as though embarrassed or afraid of what might happen if she does not contain her happiness. Let it out, I want to say to her. Instead, I stare fixedly at her mouth as though she might let me in.

"Maya had a baby."

"Did she really?"

"Yeah, it's all over Facebook. Where have you been?"

"Here," I laugh.

The sound is hollow. It hasn't occurred to me, since I emigrated, to check on the progress of my ex-classmates. It was becoming too much for me before, the endless tirade of pictures; people posing with their new cities and houses and friends at university. Some had been travelling, others training for jobs— real career jobs—that meant they could start renting poky flats of their own with their smiling partners. Every post was like another prod at my shoulder, like my mother asking what I was planning, what I was doing, when I was going to figure it out.

I take a sip of my cold coffee and welcome its strength. Men stride by Beyza and I, unsuspecting. Their language is incomprehensible to me, though this street is as narrow and notched with graffiti as any on my side of the wall.

"Oh, and I ran into Lily recently. Apparently she got off with that guy, what's his name. The posh one."

"Who?" I ask.

Beyza names a reality TV show that we once watched together.

"*What*? When?"

"She said it was right before he went on there, in a club."

"I can't believe that. Wait, so what was his name?"

"Mmn." Beyza sucks at her straw, frowning. "I can't remember."

"Oh. That's still so cool though, wow," I chortle.

Her brow tautens.

"Cool that she can say it happened, I mean."

Another breeze blows in between us, this one stronger, knocking our straws across our glasses. Beyond the single episode I tuned into with Beyza, I never got into reality TV, watching the fallout of other people's poor decisions when I could barely handle making my own. Everyone at school had been talking about it, so Beyza invited me over to give it a go. The single girls were waiting in a line to step forwards for the boys they fancied, who in turn would choose which girls they wanted to couple up with.

"This show is sexist," Beyza said, through a mouthful of popcorn, "and homophobic. Or not inclusive of non-straight people, anyway." But she made no move to turn it off, just kept crunching.

"Really?" I said, when the boy on-screen went off-piste and picked a girl who had not stepped forwards for him.

The crunching in my ear stopped, like a blockage coming unstuck.

"Well, who would you have picked?" Beyza asked, casually.

She didn't react to the answer I gave. But for weeks afterwards, she twisted the top layer of her hair up into a knot at the crown of her head, and let the locks underneath flow down her back, impossibly darker. Just like the girl in that episode had done. We didn't watch the next one.

There is a splintering sound as Beyza pokes her straw around the ice cubes at the bottom of her glass, chasing the last of the liquid.

"Shall we walk?" she suggests.

This area has become familiar to me in the last few days, since I started crossing over to spend more time with her. I can recognise pockets of it now, certain clusters of shops selling counterfeit goods and the quiet square where more coffee shops are, though I doubt I could string them together without her guiding me.

"That's the salon where my mum used to work." Beyza points at a one-story hairdressers', whose roof sags above a grubby glass front.

The women inside watch us walk past, scissors in hand.

"This is where I fell over and cut my knee, once. I had to go to hospital to get it stitched up."

"Oh god," I say, my voice echoing inside my cupped hands. "How did you do that?"

Beyza points once again, this time towards a jagged-edged step. Beyond it is a gate, green to match the vines overgrowing it and the gutter hanging off the house beyond that. "I tripped running up these steps. My cousins used to live here and I was excited, we were going to visit them. Didn't get to that day though, obviously. The blood ran all the way down and stained my white socks."

She smiles, ruefully, her eyes still fixed on the house. In them, I can see laughter and warmth, a thousand happy memories of things I can only wish I had been a part of, things that happened on the other side of those windows. But they have been boarded up now.

"What happened?" I ask.

"They moved a few years ago. Someone bought the place from them. But," Beyza shrugs, "you know how it goes."

I nod. It is the same on my side of the city; old houses like this are bought by people who intend to restore them but never do, who just let them fall into further decay. It is a pity because they are beautiful, this one in particular with its classic golden brick. Untouched. I glance at Beyza. Her cousins must have lived in virtual squalor, and still she gazes through the overgrowth with adoration. I shift closer so that my knuckles brush hers while we stand here.

"You look cute in those shorts."

"Thanks. I like your ring. That one," I say, of the chain-linked silver encircling her middle finger.

On her index finger is a chunky band and on her pinkie, two delicate ones.

"Is it new?"

"Yeah. You know I have a tattoo now, as well."

"Really?"

There is no one around. She pulls her top up to show me: a black compass high on her ribcage.

"Wow," I say. Then, "Are you bored of it yet?"

"Mean," she cries, yanking her top down again. "Don't you like it?"

"I do," I laugh, as relief and disappointment overcome me in equal measures at this first flash of bra and skin, stolen away from me again. I keep laughing or else I will blush. "It suits you. I just couldn't commit to one in case I went off it, I'd be too scared. But yours does suit you," I repeat.

She studies me. A smile creeps across her face, pearly-toothed, and my heart contracts.

"That's good to hear," she says, quietly. "I was starting to have doubts about it . . ."

We splutter, laughing, past an almost empty car park, then a coffee shop called The Olive Branch. A spray-painted hand reaches out across one whole tattered side of it towards The South. I wonder whether the proprietors approved this, or if it was done in the night like the signs on border-side bins that say 'one island' and 'the war is over'. Then we round a corner.

"There's one more thing I want to show you," Beyza says, slowing her pace.

I take in the lack of pavement, the cars parked up against dust-skirted houses. Some of their shutters are painted brilliant green, while others are peeling.

Outside a set of thin double doors, Beyza stops me. "This is my grandparents' house," she says.

"Oh." I fall back a step. With the light from inside framing her face in the hijab that I am still not used to her wearing, I feel alienated. "It's very close to the border."

She nods. "Will you remember how to get back there by yourself?"

"Yeah," I hear myself say, "I'll remember."

"And then you'll always know where to find me."

There is a pause while we look at each other, Beyza giving another of her toothless smiles. Her eyes flash bright before she hugs me, I catch my breath and just as suddenly, she disappears inside. I watch the knocker shivering against the door, despite the heat. I breathe in the old scents of cigarettes, talcum powder and bed-warmth that she has pressed upon me anew. I think, I missed her.

And yet I cannot help but wonder whose house this is really, who it belonged to before the invasion and who it probably still does now; they would not have sold it on for restoration, nor would they have received any compensation when it was taken from them. So many people still have not, decades later. I lay my

177

palm to the rough wall of the house. I might even have come to know its previous occupants, since they fled.

Twenty-Seven

I notice, when our taxi stops in traffic, a Burger King that is not a real Burger King. It can't be one. The logo looks off, the letters poorly proportioned. Conversely, the shop next door has cloned the KFC sign but is called Hungry Chicken. The pavement between it and my window is thick with people, shouting and gesticulating with shopping bags in hand. They spill out of buses into the street—these must be cast-offs from the mainland where they drive on the right—so that I might worry, if we weren't stuck edging forwards at a crawl, for their safety.

"It's always busy here," Beyza says.

"It's really busy," I agree, still staring out the window.

This is the kind of thoroughfare that should have a Pret A Manger on every corner, and a sprawling McDonald's in the middle. But it does not. Much of the population is Muslim, I suppose; if an establishment's meat is not halal, they will not do well here. Beyond that, many corporations are put off by the idea of setting up shop in an illegal state. I remember a friend of my parents' saying that his English colleagues travelled to this city, this Other Side of it, with empty suitcases just to fill them with counterfeit clothes. Nike, Adidas, Gucci; ticked T-shirts, striped trousers, chequered baseball caps. Because of the lack of regulations, they are supposed to be the best in the world.

Turning off at a roundabout, our taxi driver takes us onto a two-lane highway where the city stops dead. Billboards pop up on rusted pipes, so close together that I cannot see one behind the other.

"This is bad advertising," I say, as the road curves upwards and the windscreen fills with a mountainside, scrubbed with trees. "And it's destroying the scenery. Look at this . . ."

Beyza laughs. "How old are you?"

Turning to pull a face at her, I realise we are driving alongside the flag. It is concave, I can see from here, as I cannot from my kitchen window; it is drawn inside a 'c' of hillside with jagged rock overhanging the top, looking like it could tumble at any moment. I drag in a breath. Then the road turns towards it and we are on the other side of the ridge.

"It's so much greener up here," Beyza sighs, contentedly.

She is right; pines and cypress trees grow suddenly taller. My eyes find hers again, she smiles and at last, I exhale.

After five minutes, we come down to catch a first glimpse of the sea before it blushes back behind the trees. The road curves further around, the mountains reach out to touch the water by its shoulder and I fall back in my seat. There it is, holding my gaze for the very first time: the town where my grandfather is from.

"I told you it was nearby," Beyza says.

I have always thought of the capital as being inland, but I suppose it is not on a map. Not to Andreas or anyone else who had this most beautiful place stolen away from them. "It's more built up than I thought."

As we drive in between the first few buildings, Beyza nods. "It's all modern up here, yeah. The old town is down by the harbour. There was lots of tourism there, so they expanded it . . ."

The taxi driver glances at me in the rear-view mirror, questioning the relationship between my apparent tour guide and I, I imagine, questioning where I am from. I send my gaze out to the casinos, which appear to have had as much money devoted to their construction as the mosques, all domes and gold plating, while the surrounding apartment buildings peel as though great talons have torn down their walls. Beyza says something that I don't understand, and our driver lets us out on a roundabout. Beyond it, the buildings look squatter, the roads thinner. He drives away and the sun beats down on us.

"This way?" Beyza suggests.

With dark sunglasses on as well as her hijab, I can only see the squash-like end of her nose and her lips, subtly upturned. I feel my cheeks glow and realise that I must be smiling, too. Our footsteps echo through the backstreets.

"Do you come here a lot?" I ask her.

She leads the way with confidence down winding cobbled streets, past rows of houses with faded wooden shutters, vibrant flower boxes, leaning bikes and telephone wires criss-crossing between them. Just like in the old parts of our city, there is rust and there is rot, but there are pockets of artistry, too; ornate double doors that have been carved with intricate swirls or stained turquoise and melded into bobbling like braille.

Beyza pushes her sunglasses up her nose. "We come here to eat quite a lot. My grandparents like the fish restaurants."

As she says this, we stumble down a steep decline into the harbour.

"I can see why," I breathe.

The smell of salt fills the air. Collections of tables and chairs curl away from us in an arc while small boats nose at their legs, along with the cats, as though begging for scraps. I lift my sunglasses to see that the water beneath them is vivid blue.

"Pirate ship foam party," a man hollers on his way past us, pressing a leaflet into my hand, "This Thursday. Lunch is free."

"Thank you," I stammer.

Beyza clutches my arm and laughs. "He thinks you're a tourist," she says.

I put my sunglasses back over my eyes.

She leads the way along the water's edge, between red and white tablecloths and men hanging off the side of an old building, shouting, throwing tools back and forth. Tourists taking pictures, mothers herding their children. At the edge of the harbour, the famous castle looms. It is assured by two-thousand years of history, puffing its chest out over the sea; its wall looks like the bow of the grandest boat here.

I follow Beyza up some stone steps, uneven in size, and stop just before the ticket office. Look back. The view is like a postcard. Like a scene from one of those picturesque towns in rural Germany or Iceland, except that everyone is wearing shorts and my back is damp with sweat, not snow; the mountains are dusted brown instead of white. I think this is the most beautiful place I have ever been. I think Beyza is beautiful, too. I feel a downward tugging at the corners of my mouth as I look from her to the harbour where my grandfather—his parents, his children and perhaps even me, Jason's child—should still be living. People push past me and I let them, let Beyza make apologies for both of us in English. I keep staring until my sight blurs.

"Are you okay?" she asks me, quietly.

The sightseers who climbed past us are asking for tickets, I can hear them. They are from my side of the island. Amongst themselves, they speak my language, the language that once was spoken here. A fist closes in my stomach. I feel less like I have transgressed today, since I am not the only one visiting. But the fact that these people and I are being shepherded like tourists on our own island appals me. *Why*? Why are we playing along with this? There are still refugees from this area living on our side of the wall, with nothing. Everything they had was taken from them—illegally, according to official bodies worldwide—and yet here we are, paying for entry tickets to sites that should be ours to see.

"Dani?" Beyza says.

I blink my eyes dry. Taking the land back is not an option. No one wants another war, nothing is worth that, but it is unbelievable to me that there has still been no resolution, no reprimanding, no closure and no compensation, for the most part, for those who lost their property. There has to be *something*, doesn't there, in this modern era? Not just a quiet acceptance. What kind of message does that send to the rest of the world?

"It's not us, you know," Beyza says, softly. "The people on our side, I mean. Most of us were here before. We didn't support the invasion and we don't support whatever nationalism *he's* trying to get going now."

She jerks her head towards the horizon where sea blends into sky, and I know she is talking about the leader of the country that invaded this one. He has been a leader for far longer than anyone should, anywhere, and still he is in office. Offering houses here on this Other Side of our island to men from poor villages there, having them vote a certain way, manipulating the demographic in favour of further division, driving apart people like Beyza and I. Or so my father and great grandfather tell me.

"I know," I say.

"But you're not all angels either."

184

I look at her.

"You have to admit," she says, in response to the shock on my face, "hardly anyone on your side actually died during the war. And probably no one would have if you hadn't tried to clear us out and unify the island with—"

"A third of us lost our homes. This whole area," I say, gesturing violently over the harbour, "was *ours*."

"And half of us had to move out of The South. Our villages have been left to decay," Beyza says, her eyes bright and unflinching, "or taken over, just like yours have. We're the same," she asserts. Then, softer, "Just the same."

I drop my fists to my sides, unfurl them. A sea breeze lifts the salt to my nostrils and I wonder, for a moment, whether I am crying. I brush my fingers over my cheeks, then disguise the motion as tucking my hair back and am reminded that I cannot see Beyza's. It is hidden away inside her hijab, which is deep purple today, while mine battles like a sail against the wind. Wiry, like Paris's. Paris who is of my heritage but made me feel like an outsider with his lusting over my 'exotic' blue eyes. Beyza is 'other', but with her I feel more aware than ever of the place on this island that I am from. Perhaps too aware, though I want to fit in. I want to lay her head on my shoulder, hold her close. Our relationship is different here, more complicated than it was in England where there was no physical barrier between us, only a shared longing for this island that was home to both our families,

185

home in every sense. We felt like home to each other, and now we are pining for it as though overseas again, even though we are both here. We miss each other, I think, miss that comfort, that simplicity. We want what we had, and perhaps we can get it back.

"I'm here for you, whatever you need," Beyza says, her eyes still fixed upon me.

Falteringly, I nod. Smile at her. Our hands brush as we carry on towards the castle.

Twenty-Eight

Maria's flat is the only one on the top floor of the building. Outside it, the corridor comes around to meet the stairs in an L-shape studded with doors to storage cupboards, the flat roof and the water tank on top of it. This last door is glass. I stare out at my aunt's laundry hung on the line, so still that it seems to be staring back at me. I blink. There is no wind today, and the terrace is in full sun.

"Dani," she smiles. "Come in."

I am relieved by the fans spinning, cooling her flat.

"How are you?"

"Good," I say, as she shuts the door behind me.

"Oh, sorry." Scuttling past me, she goes into the next room to turn off the radio. Blaring pop music, just like in her car.

I smile. "That's okay. You can leave it on, if you want."

"Are you sure?" Her hand hovers over the power button, then defects to lowering the volume. "If you want to change it, let me know. You can even connect your phone."

"Really," I say, following her over the threshold.

I lose interest in the radio. The room around it is large—twice the size of my living-dining space—with not two but four sliding doors to its balcony. The shutters are up, giving a grand view over the park, level with the tops of its tallest pines and evergreens. Birds flurry between their branches.

"You can see so much from up here," I say, over the whine of a nasal voice and a prosthetic beat. "I can't believe how different this view is from mine, and you're only a floor above me."

I turn to take in the yellow sofa with its trellis-patterned cushions, the dotted leather pouffes, the potted plants and the rugs strewn over the floor and up the walls.

"You have a beautiful home."

"Thank you," Maria giggles, before falling quiet in the way that she does at mealtimes with our family.

And I realise: this is someone who has been gifted as much as I have by Andreas and Eliza. More. I suppose I haven't noticed it before because I have never been up here; on holidays, we always went to their house for dinner. Maria's paintings adorn these walls as they do her parents', though the walls themselves are not decorated like those in her childhood bedroom were. I touch my fingertips, lightly, to the edge of a canvas.

"Do you have more?" I ask her. This is what I am here for after all.

Crossing the room, she pulls a chair up to the wall and opens a high built-in cupboard. I hold her steady, smelling must and the lavender of the moth-repellent sachets inside. There is the shifting of plastic across wood before Maria passes a box down to me. Then another, and another. We are both panting when she

188

climbs down from the chair, her unruly hair even wilder than before.

"Okay," she says, casting it back.

I look at the clear plastic boxes, large and loaded with her paintings. Unlidded, they smell woody and varnished and have dates marking their corners alongside her initials; she has stored them chronologically. One by one, I flick through them. The phases she went through are clear—acrylic beaches at sunset; spray-painted night skies; ceramic masks she made for her first attempt at a university project, before failing and flailing to turn them into something more layered with canvas and mesh, for her second try which passed—right up until she found the Church. Or rather, I suppose, until the Church found her, when it knocked on her door with a clipboard and a smile.

"Do you want something to drink?"

At the sound of Maria's voice, I stir from my musing. "Yeah, please. Just some water would be good."

She starts towards the kitchen, long denim shorts washing around her thighs. I wait until I can no longer hear them to look inside the third box. The works it contains are the last she ever did, striking pictures of faceless women knelt in the palms of giant hands, of hands held together in prayer before yellow suns. Without taking my eyes off them, I shift to relieve the weight from my toes. Then I look at the final painting.

A pure blue sky is eclipsed by a hill, brown with one or two shrubs and a square white building at the top. Its sign does not need to be legible for me to know: this is a copy of the Kingdom Hall, the one that my aunt attends twice weekly. The paint is cool, with a texture like bark. I flick past it and then there is nothing, just the side of the plastic box. Maria put her paintbrushes down before going into a service one day, came out and never picked them up again.

"Here you are."

"Thanks."

The glass she gives me is ice cold.

"Did you see anything you like?"

"Yeah." Resting my drink on a side table, I sift through for one of her earlier pieces and pull it, carefully, from its box. "I really like this one."

From her perch on the arm of the sofa, Maria inclines her head. "Ah, that one?"

I nod, speechless. Judging by the date, this was a product of her sunset phase; two dark-haired girls sitting, knees to chests, on a bank overlooking the sea. With the world around them fading to shades of gold and purple, one of them leans her head on the other's shoulder, and there they stay. Of course they do. I shake myself. It is a painting.

"Take it."

"What?"

"Take it, if you want. You can keep it," Maria says.

"Oh, no. I couldn't . . ." Even as I shake my head, my grip on the canvas tightens. "Are you sure?"

"These are only things," she says, in the solemn tone she always uses to impart a teaching of the church; I have begun to recognise it.

"Thank you." Tugging my shorts down as I stand, I glance once more at her portrait of the Kingdom Hall. "I'd like to come to a service with you. Next week, maybe. If you'll still have me."

I do not have time to wonder where these words spilled out of me from before she smiles, eyes wide.

"Of course," she says, "we can go anytime."

She seals the boxes shut, and still this promise hangs between us. I tuck the girls under my arm. Past the radio pumping out rhythmic beats, I escort them, and back down the stairs to my flat.

Twenty-Nine

And then we are the two girls, Beyza and I, the only two girls in the world. She leans her head on my shoulder, just like in my aunt's painting, to hide the smile that she can no longer contain.

We are standing on the first-floor balcony of what used to serve as an inn, here on the Other Side of the city. Now it is revered as the best example of its architectural style on the island, with cafes beneath the pointed arches that frame the courtyard and traditional craft workshops up in the rooms behind us. It was renovated to include these establishments in the early nineties, apparently. After the invasion that severed our city, that made this side of it 'The North'.

I watch people coming and going from the cafes their ancestors used as stables, talking and laughing, milling around the domed prayer room in the centre of the courtyard. It is balanced upon pillars above an ablutions fountain. The design is rare, a sign next to it says; it can only be found in two places on the mainland of the country that invaded ours. This example can be traced back to the fifteen-hundreds. I cock my head. It is easy to forget, with a different, less distant invasion so palpable, that this territory was always disputed.

Beyza lifts her head from my shoulder. "Are you okay?"

"Yeah." I clear my throat, smile at her. "Good. Just looking around."

"We can go in that shop, if you want."

I follow her gaze along the sunlit gallery, past bouquets of dried flowers strung up on the wall, to a selection of slouchy handbags, feathered dream catchers and pegboards of jewellery.

"Handmade," the man inside tells me. He is quiet and stooping beneath the arched white ceiling. "You want to try?" he asks, when I pause for too long over a necklace.

It is dripping tiny beads of yellow and orange.

"Oh, no." I step back. "That's okay. I was just looking. Thank you."

He nods, backs off. I duck into the next room, where Beyza is studying glass animals and a woman who might be the proprietor's wife waits, smiling, to show me more jewellery.

"All are handmade," she says, indicating another pegboard of necklaces.

As though hearing this for the first time, I nod, point to one almost at random and say, "This is nice."

"This is copper," the woman replies.

My gaze shifts back to the beaded chain of hammered ovals. Metal, apparently, not stone as I had thought. "Copper," I echo.

She unhooks it from its peg. "You want to try?"

"You don't have to . . ." I start.

But she is already squeezing in between me and a display of trinket boxes, unclasping it. "No problem," she is saying.

Her husband comes bowing through the narrow doorway. I feel embarrassed by the damp skin under my hair as I hold it up. This woman cannot possibly want to touch it, and still she threads the chain around my neck.

"Sorry," I repeat, bending my knees to make it easier for her; she is at least a head shorter than I am.

"No problem."

"Thank you . . ."

Taking a step back, she motions to her husband who presents me with a mirror. Two cracks fracture its glass so I have to twist to see my reflection clearly. Over my shoulder, the woman watches with her lumpen nose and tawny waves of hair, shy-smiling. She and her husband both are so humble, so kind, I think again; they remind me of the waiter at that coffee shop who I suspected of flirting with Beyza. Now I see that he was not. There is a level of conscientiousness here that there is not on my side of the border. And yet. The light catches my collarbones. Copper, the element that unites us. We all have it in common, reddening the earth under our feet; this island was named for it. It feels soothingly cool to the touch.

"That suits you," Beyza's voice sounds behind me.

"I'll take it," I say. I will wear it as my countrymen wear their crosses.

We thank the couple and go back outside.

"Are you sure you're alright?" she asks, as a breeze wafts the smell of spices from a shop next door.

Several varieties make up a world map on the wall outside, stuck to the countries they are from. I fold my paper-wrapped necklace into my bag, and we continue past a selection of hanging plants to the door of a shadow puppet theatre. Here, we stop.

"Yeah," I say. "I like going around with you."

"I like you going around with me too," Beyza says. She glances over her shoulder before adding, "You can keep doing it, if you want."

"Can I?"

"Yeah." Her blush deepens.

Sensing an opening, I tilt my head. Take a breath. Feel my heart beat faster in my chest. I have never been decisive enough to do this before. It has happened many times of course, at Beyza's initiation, but not since we have been here. I lean in, lowering my eyelids just enough to catch the flash of realisation beneath hers before she pulls away. I flush, mortified.

"I'm sorry," Beyza says at once, her eyes darting with all the urgency her body lacks; her hands are rigid, curled at her sides. "I'm so sorry. I just can't do that in public here."

"It's fine," I say. The words come out sounding as stiff as her shoulders look, raised like hackles. I shrug mine. "You were always embarrassed by me, anyway."

"That's not true."

She looks again over her shoulder as a gaggle of tourists exits the puppet theatre, their voices high and loud. I bow further over the balcony, relish the burn under my fingernails as I dig them into the bannisters. I am not looking, not even at Beyza.

"I'm not embarrassed by you," she insists, as the group moves on. "It was my parents back in England and here, it's *this*."

A stubborn moment passes. I glance sideways at her, her hijab pinched between her thumb and forefinger.

"Not everyone here is as progressive as they are in London. To be honest, even in London . . ."

The people below us distend into obscurity as I stare and do not blink.

"But I've never stopped thinking about you."

"I haven't stopped thinking about you either," I hear myself say, treacherously soft amidst the bustle.

I make no attempt to take the statement back. It is true. Whenever I have tried to move on from Beyza—even recently, with Paris—I have failed to get her out of my head, my heart or wherever it is that she waits to be compared to anyone new. Are they taller than her, shorter than her? Do they laugh just as easily, but smile to their fullest only when made to feel special

196

enough? Do they make me feel special enough? Is it possible that they could want to make a go of things with me, with the full throttle force that she did, until we crashed and burned? Will I ever experience that feeling of lifting off the ground with someone again? I shake my head. I know I am in dangerous territory here, that I have been since running into my ex a few weeks ago. Half a decade ago, we were on, indefinitely. Then we were most definitely off. And now?

"If you can stand sneaking around a bit longer, I would like to keep seeing you," Beyza says. "Like that, I mean. Just . . . carefully."

The breath shocks from my lungs. "I'd like that too," I say.

And at last, the danger is over.

"I wish I could kiss you," my girlfriend says.

I smile, my flush forgotten, and we descend into the courtyard.

Thirty

A tide of colour rolls downhill to the Kingdom Hall, while another surges up from the plain beneath it. They meet with a mismatching clash at the doors; there is noise and wind and the spindrift catches me, makes me squint. Even my aunt is dressed in yellow. The only force brighter than she and the rest of the congregation is the sun, shining down on their attire that is more fit for a wedding than a funeral, for once. I hadn't realised how accustomed I was to the head-to-toe black clothing of my family, their friends. I must look out of place yet again, wearing mine here. Reluctant and drab. I try to smile extra brightly to make up for it. Maria greets her friends in English, as she did that day in the mountains.

A man in a three-piece suit welcomes us at the doors.

"Wonderful," he says, when Maria tells him who I am. His American accent is more mawkish than my mother's. "Good to meet you, Daniela. I'm Saxon."

I mumble my thanks. The sunlight gleams off his head.

There are patterns and chuckles and claps on the back, then nothing. I look up, frown. Suddenly it is all quite underwhelming. Through the doors, the congregation's clothing remains the brightest feature in sight. No stained glass windows or crosses adorn the walls; we are in a room that is as plain and boxy inside as it looks on the outside. The air is clear of candle smoke, and smells stagnant. There are no crosses even on anyone's neck. As I realise this, the copper weighs around mine and I touch it, then take a seat beside Maria in a retiree's chair close to the front. Our whereabouts burns through my mind like neon in the darkest night.

"Welcome, friends. Brothers and Sisters, thank you for joining us. I would like us to talk today about the nine puzzle pieces to a happy family."

Behind Saxon, behind his podium, a PowerPoint pops up with nine empty squares inside one big one.

"We'll fill them in as we go of course, but let's start with the central piece. Unselfish love," he says.

Murmurs sound over the hum of the projector, someone fumbling for the next slide.

"In order to be a good wife," Saxon goes on, "what must a woman be?"

"Respectful," members of the congregation infer from Colossians. "She should speak highly of her husband. She should make the family home a place of comfort and protection. She should instil the values of the Church in her children."

"Wonderful," he replies. "Very good."

Women lower their ringed hands smiling.

"And how can a husband honour his wife?"

"He can praise her. Reassure her. Remind her of Jehovah's great qualities and help to correct her negative thinking."

Once again, Saxon commends those who answer him. "Just think to yourself," he says, "'when was the last time I said something nice to my wife?'"

At this, a man in front of me leans into the ear of a bristling woman. Her shoulders remain rigid as he whispers, then resigns himself to the back of his chair. It creaks.

"Marriage and children are precious gifts from our creator. He wants us to have a happy family life, so by means of this sacred book he has given us guidance that can make our relationships better. Problems arise at home. Perhaps you live in a household with mixed beliefs. Perhaps you have become entrenched in bad habits. You are a wife going shopping and spending money without consulting your husband, for example. Perhaps there has been a breach of trust, a husband watching pornography, or perhaps you are struggling to train your children. Jehovah can help you not only to cope with these things, but to overcome them. So. We'll sing song number thirty-four, 'Walking in Integrity', and then move on to Watchtower Study to see how."

The room rises around me and I start to my feet on the delay of a shadow. There is the swelling of orchestral music, the drawing in of a unanimous breath and then they are singing, the whole congregation, including my aunt. Her tunelessness startles me. I look sideways to see that her sparkly-lidded eyes are bright regardless, her smile wide as she sings without needing the words. I try to mouth them, picking the skin around my thumbnails at my sides.

"Last week we discussed not stirring up competition," Saxon says, resuming his place at the podium. "This week we'll build on that with Article Twenty-Nine, and learn to 'rejoice in our own progress' rather than comparing ourselves with others. I look forward to hearing your well-prepared comments. If we could start with a reading of paragraph one please, John . . ."

As a younger man stands up to read from Chapter Six, my eyes dart between the uncapping of pens and opening of notebooks all around me. Maria has written numbers in the margin of her page and appears poised to count down them with a marking pen. I feel like the only student who has not done their homework. Fearful of being picked on, I bow my head.

"You can look at mine," she whispers.

"Thank you, John, for that reading," Saxon's voice sounds. "Why does Jehovah not compare us with others?"

A child answers this question, her blonde curls bouncing as she jumps up and down. "He loves us for our va-ri-e-ty."

The adults who fuss over her speak out afterwards. Paragraph two: why is it not good to compare ourselves with others? Paragraph three: what spiritual progress have we made? Paragraph five: what should parents avoid?

"Comparing their children," the girl's mother says, draping an arm over her daughter's shoulders. Beside her, a boy of about ten tugs at his bow tie.

We hear paragraph six, then Psalm 131:1-2.

Saxon nods. "Thank you, John. And what can parents learn?"

A green-blazered man clears his throat. "Sometimes the goals we set for our children are too high, especially in the west. Saying 'you can accomplish anything you set your mind to' sets unrealistic expectations."

As everyone nods, I glance at Maria and think of the wide white canvases she used to set her brushes to.

"Absolutely," Saxon responds, "and this is where quite a few of our puzzle pieces come in."

He turns over his shoulder to the squares which by now have been filled in with Forgiveness, Honesty, Patience and Obedience. "We as parents all know how tough puberty can be. We remember."

We chuckle.

"Brother Alan said, 'Because of my obsessively comparing myself with other boys, I started feeling attracted to them. It wasn't until later in my youth that I developed an attraction to females. Homosexual feelings are now just a part of my past.'"

Saxon pauses for breath and I stop chuckling.

"As parents, what could we train a child like Brother Alan to do?"

"Learn to control his urges so he doesn't act on them. Corinthians 6:18 says 'Flee from sexual immorality . . . Whoever practises sexual immorality is sinning against his own body.'"

"Resist the urge to focus on his body image. And avoid comparing himself to others physically. 'Man sees what appears to the eyes, but Jehovah sees into the heart.' Samuel 16:7."

"I would tell a boy like Brother Alan truthfully, 'Men who practice homosexuality . . . will not inherit God's Kingdom.' And a girl the same. 'God gave them over to disgraceful sexual passion, for their females changed the natural use of themselves into one contrary to nature'. Romans 1:26."

"As per our puzzle," Saxon says, "We must communicate with our children. But we must also 'pursue peace with all people', as instructed by Hebrews 12:14. We must apply patience and, for our next piece, Mildness."

The air cools. It recedes from my skin, leaves me naked and damp, my mouth open. But no sound goes out. None comes in either; the room revolves and I raise a hand to my head. I am sure I have heard the next question asked already.

"How can a husband honour his wife?"

The answer is different this time. "He can listen when she speaks. Refrain from comparing her with other women for her looks or her skills."

"So no, 'I wish you could cook like your mother'. Right?"

Laughter resounds.

"How can elders help those who have a tendency to compare themselves with others?"

Saxon reads once more from his podium. "Sister Hanuni said, 'Elders asked me to encourage some Sisters who needed help. These assignments made me feel needed . . . I now treasure my place in Jehovah's organisation.'"

The bar of my chair digs into my back. So, women must be needed, must prove useful to others, to become valid as individuals even unto themselves. And people shouldn't be given help solely for their own sake. My aunt's face shines up to Saxon's podium, bathing in the light of his message. I crane up at him, brow furrowed, and try to understand it. Perhaps motivation does not matter when it results in aid, which is all-important. Everyone here could have lent their hands to each other for entirely selfish reasons, and still built this supportive community.

We run into Eziamaka guiding a hunched, grey-haired woman outside. "Good service today," she beams.

While my aunt speaks with her and the stranger, I look around for the rest of their friends. Half the congregation has disappeared already, in clouds of dust from the sun-baked earth beyond the doors. Rose must have gone with them. I think I glimpse the back of Elena alongside a middle-aged woman who is not Lim. Perhaps her mother, Lim's friend. Then they are gone and we are shuffling out after them.

Shielding my eyes, I root for my sunglasses. The world basks in their warm tint, and another stranger appears before me. Eziamaka's laughter stops in my ears.

"Hi, David," Maria says.

He lowers himself from his great height with a gentle cock of his head. The hair upon it is cropped to a cloud-like haze. "Are you well?"

"Yeah." She smiles up at him, timidly, thoughts racing across her eyes as they were mine just moments ago. "And you?"

"I am very well, thank you."

"Goodbye, all. See you on Thursday," Eziamaka calls, still bracing the older woman with one meaty forearm.

"Bye," the three of us say, then look back at each other.

I become aware of my hands at my sides and move one, needlessly, to the strap of my bag. Maria tucks back a tangle of her hair. David looks too tall again, like he should be teetering in the warm breeze, and yet he is still. Smiling at her. They are drawn to each other, I can feel it, longing to lean in and kiss and touch one another as lingeringly as their eyes do, and yet they do not.

"Well. Good to see you," David says.

"You too," Maria replies.

Dust rises between their feet.

I return home and to Jw.org. Dating is a step towards marriage, it says, not something recreational.

'Couples who are dating can avoid being alone in tempting situations. They may choose to take such reasonable precautions as staying in the company of a wholesome group or a suitable chaperone.' No sexual act is permitted before vows are exchanged.

I think of the gleam in Maria's eyes when she said no, that she was not seeing anyone, and I realise: her feelings are at odds with her faith. I sit back from my phone. Religion comes between Beyza and I continually. It always has—it was because of her parents' beliefs that we could never progress before—and so I decide that this will be my first and last service. I will not go back to the Kingdom Hall with my aunt, but I will do better than our family by respecting her faith. If everyone respected each other's feelings and didn't make facts of their own, I think, religious or not, North or South, the world might be a better place. Somewhere I could live both without doubts *and* with Beyza.

Thirty-One

On my next day off, I sleep in a little. Open my eyes, pull my sheets up around me and flick the air conditioning off at the wall. The room is so cold, I feel that I should be covered in dew. Eight a.m., my phone says. In the absence of a clock, I have been sleeping with it next to my head. This is terrible, Eliza tells me. I drop it back to the bedside table.

Swinging my feet to the floor, I pull on a black T-shirt and a pair of 'gym' shorts that I haven't even worn to sleep, since coming here. The evenings are too hot. I tug them down as I leave the cave of my over-cooled room, and pad into the kitchen where there are no curtains to preserve my modesty.

The kettle boils quietly in its old age. While waiting for it, I spoon two scoops of coffee into a rickety cafetiére and lean back against the counter. I try not to think about Paris pushing me into it. I don't need to, I remind myself, as the flag of the Other Side watches over my shoulder, a steady presence. The water reaches boiling point with a 'click'. I pour it into the cafetiére, balance the press-top on, replace the kettle. There is silence.

And then the siren.

It takes me a moment to decipher the noise, a high-pitched whine piercing through my walls at intervals. It is muffled so that it could be a car skidding too fast around a corner. Then another car, and another car. It could be the megaphoned voice of someone crawling the streets, selling potatoes from their van. It could be a call-to-prayer. But there are no mosques near to where I live.

My hands feel weightless as I walk out of the kitchen, past the table and chairs to the balcony doors. Beyond them, everything is still. No birds fly above the park's trees, no neighbours stand out in their gardens.

Breath held, I put my hand to the door. Slide it open. Freeze, like the air conditioning is upon me again. I fall back gasping and the heat pursues me. I can hear it now, the sound slinking all the way up and down like a captive animal, turning at each corner of its cage, anticipating a strike. It is everywhere, rising and falling in and out of time with itself across streets, not intermittent or muffled at all. It is unmistakable, even to someone who has not lived through a war. My ears ring instinctively.

I stumble backwards into the table, look down. My hands have turned from limp to trembling. Why is no one bursting out into the street? Where are they? Where should I be?

I think of my year three classroom, the black and yellow posters we pinned to the walls while we were learning about the Blitz. 'Blinds down or bombs away!' I remember writing on mine, in a cheerful scrawl. I see the silver shells I coloured in, humming along to a song that was stuck in my head, with my favourite metallic marker. I consider wrenching my shutters down but it is daylight, and pilots have GPS systems now; they don't need to see their targets to secure them anymore. Nor do they need to fly planes.

The stairs fall away beneath my bare feet. My breasts ache but I do not stop, do not slow down. The siren arches higher in the echoing stairwell. My ears and eyes brim with terror and I slip down the bottom step, then tear out of the building.

The world is a droning hot haze. There is no time to turn back for anything, barely time even to break through my great aunt's gate and cry, "*Grandmother.*"

Slowly, she turns to face me. Rita's darkened doorway frames her frown.

"Grandmother," I persist, the terror spilling out and down my cheeks, "what is it? What do we do?"

"What do we do?" she repeats, showing no signs of urgency.

Shehani emerges from behind her. She bids me good morning and proceeds to water the plants, as if there is nothing to be heard but the crickets.

I stare after her, agog. "*What . . ?*"

"What is the matter, my love? Ah," Eliza says, her eyes widening, "the siren?"

The absurdity of my panic collapses in on me like a parachute. I am unable to breathe, unable to find my way out from under the swathes of coloured fabric; my classmates have dropped the corners and gone back inside without me.

"Today is the anniversary. Of the invasion," my grandmother says.

And just like that, the siren stops. Water trickles audibly from Shehani's can; a car moves off from its parking; crickets hum in unison. I hear all these sounds as if they have just started up, still with a ringing in my head.

"You didn't know?"

"No," I breathe, as the adrenaline floods me. I become aware of the dirt shards digging into my feet, my loose breasts and tiny shorts. I fold my arms across my chest.

"They play this siren every year," my grandmother explains, "to remind us."

I suppose I had no way of knowing. As a child, I couldn't come here until the end of July. I spent the first half of the month stuck in school, staring out the window and fantasising about my upcoming visit to this family, this city, year after year. I never made it in time. I feel foolish now, like an outsider, not someone who knows comprehensively these streets that the tanks rolled down, on this day not so many years ago. They headed for the palace, where the president was meeting with a group of foreign children. The time was around eight-twenty, as it is now. I know this, and still I feel ignorant. I feel perhaps the smallest, most sheepish bit lucky, and guilty for it.

"Well." I manage a hollow laugh. "They reminded us."

Squeezing my shoulder, Eliza chuckles. But there is pain in her eyes, too.

Thirty-Two

"Hallo, hallo," my grandfather greets me, rising from his place on Rita's sofa.

"Good morning," my great grandfather echoes, though he does not move from his.

I give him a wave and Andreas a kiss on each cheek. Then I sink into an armchair directly opposite Rita's. Keep sinking. At eye level, her forehead stretches even further up her head. I can see the angle that her swollen legs are crushed at between the coffee table and her chair, how uncomfortable she must be, and I cannot escape her rolling stare. Since meeting me at the door, Eliza has been in and out of the kitchen, calling coffee orders to Shehani. Now she is faffing with chairs, performing a headcount of our immediate family. The one member who is missing still counts. She will always count, Katerina, *to* us and against *them*, though she may never be accounted *for*. Eliza lowers her finger. Andreas and George have resumed their fiery political hissing, charring the edges of each other's words before sitting back in inevitable agreement, and still I feel bound by the silence of my great aunt's gaze. Tucking my hair back, I look to Maria, who is perched on the end of the sofa next to George.

"Hallo, Dani. How are you?"

"Good," I say, "and you?"

"Good, thank you." She giggles.

Her eyes are half closed, covered with a nude sparkle. Her every syllable is stretched thinner and higher-pitched than usual, as it always is around her parents. Like something fragile, something that should not be pushed or prodded at or else it might break, so you have to be gentle with it. Eliza has to be gentle with it. I understand this now.

"Okay," my grandmother says, coming to sit down at last.

The chair she settles on looks like it belongs in a castle bedchamber with its upholstered seat cushion, its ornately carved wooden legs and its low, snaking back. She brings a plastic fan with her, the air grazing my nose and cheek.

George takes a swipe at Andreas's elbow and they are off once again. I sit tight and try to feign interest in their debate, to remain as sparingly reactive as my aunt is; I, too, have things to hide now.

"So, my love," Eliza addresses me.

The copper ovals weigh heavily around my neck. "Yes?"

"You had a more peaceful rest this morning?"

Maria gives another tinkling laugh.

"I was telling her," my grandmother explains, "about how you ran downstairs, you didn't know it was the anniversary."

"Oh," I say.

"She was," Eliza reiterates to my aunt, this time miming the action, "*running*. She was very scared."

213

At this, all three of us affect laughter. A beat passes, we look at each other. Then we look down at our hands.

The rattling of cups on saucers precedes Shehani's entrance into the room.

"Daniela is here, Shehani," Eliza says, quickly.

"Hallo," Shehani mumbles. She puts her tray down without looking at me.

Frowning, I watch her flee the room and notice Atay in the corner, also watching her. I take a sip of my coffee for warmth.

"You know," my grandmother goes on, clearing her throat, "There is another anniversary five days from now, so you are prepared. At five-thirty in the morning."

"Right," I say. "Thanks."

Shehani returns, this time with a cake. Plates are passed around, compliments given to her, the chef. The conversation moves on. It is going to be forty degrees today, my great grandfather warns us. Hotter. I speak little and only when spoken to, across the shuttered wall from my aunt like a mirror, doing the same. At the head of the coffee table, Rita wilts in her armchair like a dying monarch while Shehani serves her, loyal to the last, from a neon spoon. Another Sri Lankan sponge. At first, I savour the buttery melt of it in my mouth. But as we sit here, Eliza giggling and babbling, giddy as ever to be surrounded by her family, my tongue begins to curl. Shehani is sniffling, like she has the flu and should be in bed. To think that I was affronted by her greeting me without her usual enthusiasm is an embarrassment. If I were half as sick as she looks now, I would never have gone into work. Not even at Oxfam, I think, with a pang. Of course, I didn't live in Oxfam's back room, didn't rely on its good graces for my right to remain in England.

A half-chewed mouthful rolls from Rita's tongue.

"She is getting worse," Eliza says, remorsefully, as it lands on her plate with a slap that makes me tense, wrinkle my nose.

"This is almost too much now, for the girls."

Shehani looks up from dabbing at Rita's chin, her eyes as wet as the sound. Was she sniffling like that while she baked the cake? I jab my fork into my gums, and this selfish thought gets lost in the rush of blood I can taste. Poor Shehani. I hope she is okay, I correct myself. Then I send my eyes over her shoulder to Atay. She is the only one of us not eating. She is watching Shehani so closely that it makes even me feel bored into, and I have to look away from her, too.

"Any plans for the next few days?" Eliza asks.

I gulp down a cloying mouthful. "I'm going to get trained for my first evening shift at work," I say. I don't mention that I am going to see my girlfriend across the border.

Maria says, "I may see my friends later today, or tomorrow . . ." Or some other vague time that shimmers out of sight at the end of her sentence. She doesn't specify which friends, where

215

she met them in the first place or where she will, most likely, meet them again.

And Eliza does not ask. "Good," she says, simply, ignoring her watchful father and her grumbling husband. "Very nice."

Newly united in our secrecy, Maria and I smile and lower our eyes, and we all fall into silence. Above the drone of the fans, the only sound is of Shehani, sniffling and clearing her throat.

Later, I lie stretched across my bedsheets on the phone to my mother. Do I want anything from England, she has called to ask.

"Anything that'll fit in *my* suitcase," she clarifies. "Your father is planning to fill his with all the Byzantine history books he can get his hands on. Where he continues to find any that he hasn't got stored out there already, I don't know."

Behind her sigh is affection; she first fell in love with my father while he was studying this subject at Goldsmiths University. She had elected to read History and Literature, with longer hair and a Boston twang that has since become more subtle. He had long hair, too, but no beard yet. They smiled a lot. I have studied the pictures.

With the fan whirring above me, I feel my head grow heavy. I am more relaxed than I was earlier, watching the information I let slip to my grandparents, and somehow I forget that my mother might be just as reactive.

216

"*What*?" she snaps, at the mention of Maria's Kingdom Hall. "You went there?"

My eyes fly open. "Only once," I try to reassure her.

But it is too late. Deborah is shouting and whispering at once into the phone, "You will send your grandparents to early graves. What were you thinking? You can never repeat this, never go back there. Do you understand me? Never. Your aunt should know better than to take you. You can't trust those people. Especially her."

"What does that mean?" I ask, appalled.

"Dani . . ." There follows a shifting of breath, like my mother is looking over her shoulder before she murmurs, "There was an incident after our visit last year."

"An incident?" I swing my legs from the bed, swap the phone into my other hand.

"Yes. With Rita, Shehani. And Maria," my mother says.

Thirty-Three

Atay did not exist yet, not as a need or even as an idea for the household. Shehani and Rita were getting along fine, just the two of them. Not as well as they had, perhaps, back when Rita had engaged more. When Shehani had handed her a glass of cold water on a hot day, and she had nodded her quiet thanks. When the world news had depicted warfare and heat waves, and she had asked Shehani about Sri Lanka, what things were like where she was from. When she had helped Shehani learn the local language by repeating words and phrases, despite the fact that they could communicate in English; Rita had wanted to increase Shehani's prospects.

"For when I am gone," she had said.

But she still was not gone. Years had passed, years of sitting and waiting so patiently that it was as if Rita thought she might be rewarded with death, like a child who had behaved well. It was funny how people regressed with age, Shehani thought. By now, Rita had all the simplicity of mind and lack of obligation of a toddler. And yet her body was shutting down. First it had been her heart, broken by Elias's death. Then her will; she would not work, would not walk, would not do anything but wait until her time on earth was up, so she could be with him again. Of course, this had affected her spine. She had terrible pains in her legs, which Eliza's doctor suggested might be the result of a herniated disc. Rita was too sedentary, he had said; the disc was probably pressing on her sciatic nerve and she needed to walk, to stretch it out. The family had pleaded with her—Shehani, too—but she would not listen, nor would she let another doctor look at her. She had walked even less. She had grown bitter with pain. Fewer of her friends had come calling, and so her mind had also suffered. Shehani could not stimulate her as those politicians and professors and pathologists had.

So she cooked, and Rita ate. She put the television on, and Rita watched it, though she no longer shouted and gesticulated from her armchair as she had. Things were fine. Until the incident.

Shehani had made spiced lentils. She was sitting on the sofa adjacent to Rita, spooning them into her mouth while the news bellowed; Rita's hearing had worsened since she had refused treatment for an ear infection, months earlier. Her fork clattered to her plate, then onto the rug, splattering turmeric. Shehani leapt to her feet. That would never come out, she dismayed, even as she started towards the kitchen for some cleaning spray. Stopped. Looked back from the doorway. Rita was clearing her throat. She was doing it in an experimental way, as though testing the bounds of something she did not understand, with one hand on her collarbone and the other gripping her plate.

"Rita?" Shehani said, softly, "are you okay?" She stepped closer.

Rita's knuckles were white. She cleared her throat again, then gave a louder cough. It erupted into gasping, lentils spraying over the chair, the coffee table, the floor as she folded over herself, both hands at her chest now, trying to fill it with air.

"Rita," Shehani cried, the cleaning forgotten. She dropped to her knees next to Rita's and urged her, "What? What is it?" as soothingly as she could stand to, until Rita sagged against the arm of her chair.

With a straining effort, Shehani shunted her upright. She laid her hand on Rita's forehead while Rita's eyes rolled shut, then took her face between both palms.

"No. Please, stay awake. Eyes open."

The stubby eyelashes flickered. The eyes behind them were glazed, glancing this way and that, as if this was not where they had been before they closed, just seconds ago. Between laboured breaths, Rita groaned like an animal. Her hands went to her stomach.

"Are you sick?" Shehani fretted. Was it the lentils? She felt the warm mush beneath her kneecaps.

Rita's hands returned to her chest, one on top of the other this time, more clutching than they had been before. Urgency bloomed in her eyes. Shehani's widened at the sight of it. She shrank backwards, stumbled to her feet and then out onto the veranda.

"Help, help me . . . Maria," she cried, at the sight of a familiar face.

A startled look crossed it. Maria was on her way out to meet some friends. To meet David, who was new to their congregation. This was the first time he had initiated a meeting, since their exchange of shy smiles across the Kingdom Hall. She had dressed in flowery black trousers and a top that fitted her closely, but not so closely as to be provocative, she hoped. She wanted to make the right impression.

"Come quickly, please. I think your aunt is having a heart attack."

"*What*?" Maria rushed inside to see for herself.

Time stopped with the threshold at her heels. Darkness started. Sweat mottled the smell of dried spices. She recognised what Shehani did not: the swelling in Rita's feet, in her ankles and legs, was a sign of acute kidney failure, not of a heart attack. For a moment, this knowledge stunned her. But she and her brother had spent hours here as children, reading the many books while their parents were out. Jason had immersed himself in Elias's history section, while Maria had been drawn to Rita's old medical journals. She had liked them for their diagrams, which she would trace over, colour in or try to copy as exactly as she could, the budding artist that she was. Her aunt had crooned over her shoulder, ever encouraging. She remembered the images of people suffering from what Rita was now—the symptoms of fatigue, confusion, nausea, weakness, chest pains—and she remembered what must happen next if her aunt were to be saved.

Then time started again.

'For the holy spirit and we ourselves have favoured adding no further burden to you except these necessary things: to keep abstaining from things sacrificed to idols, from blood, from what is strangled, and from sexual immorality. If you carefully keep yourselves from these things, you will prosper.'

Maria had just covered this act in Watchtower Study. She looked from Rita to Shehani, who was lurching from terror to tears to screeching at her to do something, call someone, stop standing there like that. Did she want her aunt to die? No, Maria did not want Rita to die, any more than she imagined Shehani wanted to watch the light leave her work permit, her rights or her life here in this country, where she felt safe and could earn enough money to feed her whole family back home. And build them a house. She wanted to send her daughter to university. Of course she was crying, for herself and her dreams, never mind the fact that Rita might never have any again.

Maria was trembling when she reached for the phone. She was saying the Lord's Prayer that He might have mercy, grant her aunt everlasting life. Again, Shehani shouted at her to pick up the

222

phone. Again, Maria extended her hand, hesitated, and pulled it back. Behind her, Rita's breathing was ragged.

"She needs an ambulance," Shehani insisted, not understanding.

If there were to be any chance of forgiveness—because Rita had not practised—she could 'eat' no one else's blood. That might not save her even in this life. She was old and weak, willing her body to give out every day.

"An ambulance," Maria repeated.

At the sound of her aunt choking, instinct made her grab the phone.

At the same moment, Shehani cried, "Hold on," and ran from the flat, leaving Rita on the floor to writhe and gasp.

The phone hit the wall as Maria dropped down beside her.

"I'm with you," she sobbed, without looking over her shoulder.

There was no time to call for help now, nor any way of telling where Shehani had gone. Maria was dimly aware of doors slamming, footsteps sounding. Otherwise there was only her aunt, shuddering in her arms.

The life was almost out of her when the ambulance came, moments later. Maria shocked upright. Shehani and George were standing, panting, in the doorway, backed by the blur of blue lights. She felt her tears illuminated. She fell out of the way of the

223

paramedics with their scrubs and their stretcher, and watched them carry her aunt away.

Rita was kept alive, but never as haltingly well as she had been before, and so Atay was brought in to help look after her. No one was sure what would have happened, if Shehani hadn't made it to George's in time, whether Maria's hesitation would have held. Or not. But it was agreed that she should never be left alone with Rita again. Eliza was fearful of losing her mother figure, as she had lost her mother. Even more than that, she fears losing her daughter.

Thirty-Four

The sun is dipping below the flags of the old city when I arrive. Girls in flat shoes are padding home, shopping bags in hand. Women in heels are coming out to replace them, dressed in airy clothing that covers their limbs and expensive-smelling perfume. I shrink into my T-shirt and shorts. Am I too old not to have progressed? The H&M sign sticks out from the shops ahead of me, accusatory-red. Stopping outside Chest, I stare across the cobbles. The 'H', the ampersand and the 'M' stare back at me, and I feel as much like backing away as I did from Maria's car just now. Thankfully, she was pulling in from her workday as I was leaving for mine.

"I have my first evening shift," I told her, feigning regret as best I could.

She was wearing her sunglasses and I was squinting, though there was no need to anymore. The gravel met Eliza's car with a grumble and I got in with her, got away.

"Daniela."

I turn my head. Chris is waving a long lighter at me from inside Chest, his eyebrows high up his bald head. Stepping inside, I see that the tables around him are taken up with drinkers already.

"Anna has called in sick," he says, returning a candle to one of them lit. "Let's get started. Stephanie will train you." Lighting another, he nods at the bar.

I feel the flames as I walk towards it, burning my ears. I am breathing Stephanie's body spray before she looks up at me. It is sickly sweet, suffocating. The lines around her eyes are impossibly thin.

"Hallo," she greets me, in English. As if I am one of our customers, here on a holiday.

I try not to sound too keen as I reply in her language. "Hi. How are you?"

"I'm fine." She smiles thinly, tapping at the till with her glossy fake nails.

"That looks hard," I laugh, uncertainly.

She stops.

"Using the touch screen, I mean. With long nails like that. I think I'd struggle," I say. But then I wouldn't know, would I?

Stephanie raises her eyebrows and continues tapping, after a moment. "I'm used to it."

I nod, the sound filling me with relief. "So, what should I do?"

"With what?"

"This is my first late shift. Chris said you'd train me."

Stephanie tucks back a perfectly curled lock of her hair. "Train you? Okay. I mean, it's basically the same. Just take orders, clear glasses."

226

I glance around the low-lit room, hesitantly.

"Here." With another tight smile, she plucks a receipt from the jaws of the till and stuffs it into a shot glass. "You can take this to Table Eight, see if they want to pay by card or cash."

I do as she says.

On my way back, someone stops me and I take an order from his table.

"What have we got?"

"Two pints of Carlsberg, two doubles of Jack Daniels," I report back to Stephanie, "and—"

"Neat?"

"Oh." As if the customer might sign me the answer, I look back at him. "I don't know."

She takes the whiskey down from its shelf, but doesn't uncap it. My throat burns.

"Okay. What else?"

"A gin and tonic."

"Did you ask which gin?"

"Yes. That one," I say, releasing a breath.

There is a resounding ring as Stephanie turns a glass up by her talons. Through its bowl, they look even longer. "And which tonic?"

"Erm . . ."

Her shoulders sag. "You'll have to go back and ask. With whiskey, some people want ice. For gin, we have a selection of tonics. Fever-Tree. There's Aromatic, Mediterranean, Elderflower, Indian." She steps aside to reveal a fridgeful under the back bar. "Okay?"

As I retrace my steps between mismatching chairs, I am struck by the differing etiquettes around caffeine and alcohol; customers have to request sugar syrup and plant milk twists to their coffees, while bar staff must anticipate every stir and shake of the drinks they serve. Not that I miss my job as a barista in London, I remind myself. I would rather go back to working at Oxfam, where it meant more to consider my service.

I return to the bar with an order for one Jack Daniels on the rocks and a gin with Light tonic. Stephanie pushes a bowl of popcorn at me.

"Thanks, I'll get on those. You can take this to them."

"But . . ." The topmost piece, like a floret of cauliflower, tips down the mound. "They didn't order any popcorn."

Stephanie frowns. "They ordered *beer*," she says, enunciating again like I might not understand her. "The salt should make them drink faster so they order some more."

"Does that work?" I ask, disbelieving. Though now that I think of it, I see popcorn on the tables in most bars.

Stephanie shrugs. "Hopefully. We want their money, don't we?"

So it is not a generous offering. I balance the bowl on my fingertips. It is underhanded, I feel, to parch the money from

228

people's pockets while smiling and appearing though I am doing something nice, something I don't have to. It is not charity. When the group smiles up at me, gratefully, I think again of Oxfam. I wish I was still there, handwriting price tags and humming along to Travis, content in the knowledge that I was doing *good* work, even if not *the* work I would be once my life shed its fat and took on an adult shape. That felt nice.

"Table Seven," Stephanie says, pushing another bowl of popcorn across the bar.

Head bowed, I deliver it.

Thirty-Five

"It's more developed over here," Beyza declares.

It is the first time she has crossed over to my side of the city. We step out from under the flags of the old part and into the square, where once there were protests and now people picnic on heat-resistant benches, the glass towers beyond them standing tall. I try to see these modern buildings through my girlfriend's eyes; they cut above the dust and the palms, and the blaring traffic becomes jumbled and daunting, nonsensical. I glance sideways. Being with Beyza when she is intimidated, when I can sense the prickles on the back of her neck as groups of strange boys swagger by, makes me feel uneasy. She has always been the bolder of the two of us. Now that we have swapped roles, I am anxious to make this day good for her, as she has made so many for me.

We walk hand in hand to the taxi booth. My palm glows with warmth, and I don't mind that it is sweating because Beyza doesn't mind showing me this affection, here, in public. People look, but I don't care. She hasn't done it since we were teenagers. She turns to face me when I give our driver another girl's name.

"That's the beach," I smile, hastily.

She nods and the beads on her bikini strap flash beneath her top, jade-green.

The car is long and thin, and smells of an old man's smoking. Not like my aunt's, whose scent is masked by other, lighter fragrances so that it is almost quite pleasant. This smell is putrid and soggy, like tobacco has been chewed up, spat out and trampled to mulch under the feet of every passenger. Nose wrinkled, I look in the rear-view mirror and start. This is the same man who drove me home from my failed first date with Paris. Blushing, I avert my gaze, as if he might remember. But not before I see that he is staring at Beyza.

She, I realise, is taking off her hijab.

A horn blasts and our driver swerves, then surges onto the highway. I catch my breath. Apparently unbothered, Beyza shakes her hair loose, smiles. She folds her hijab into her bag, a black and white chequered rucksack stamped with the Vans logo. I release the handle of my door. This is the bag that she and a few others had at school, a very select few others who listened to the kind of churlish, grating music that was at once outlandish and cool, who 'forgot their PE kit' in favour of smoking and were both outcast and awed for their loss of virginity. Everyone was so concerned with how they fit in, socially, jostling elbows and treading on toes in a constant battle for higher standing. The hierarchy was fragile, and the threat of it shifting caused feverish nail-biting. Somehow, Beyza had existed outside of it all. Perhaps because she was quiet and non-committal, yet kind to everyone. Perhaps because she cared too little about what they thought, or perhaps she was just so different that she could not be measured by the same increments they were. *We* were. In any case, I smile as I look at her rucksack, remembering. It was that steady, offbeat assurance that drew me to her back then, when it seemed like everything and everyone else could be shaken, and she could not. Beyza was steadfast.

She squeezes my hand when our driver makes yet another maniacal lane change, and I marvel at the length of her rich brown hair. I want to feel locks of it pour through my fingers like sand.

In half an hour, we are at the beach. Beyza's eyes widen at the sum of money I owe the driver.

"It'll be worth it," I say, hopefully.

We cross a road lined with palm trees and start down a path between two coffee shops. Behind us, there is a roar to drown out the music playing in both. I follow Beyza's gaze to the chain-link fence beyond the car park, beyond the plain of a salt lake that has dried up for the summer, to a line of commercial jets. One has just taken off. The sun catches its back.

"Oh. Are we next to the airport here?" Beyza frowns.

"Yeah. It's actually really cool," I try to buoy her, but my voice sounds meek in the engine's wake.

It is more humid here than in the city, so there is a sensation like swimming before we have dipped our toes in the water. The nails on Beyza's are painted chipped black, while mine remain bare. On a sunbed, I fold them under my knees. I have always loved this beach. The sand is golden and the waves are broad, but not too high. Blue sunbeds stud the space, backed by café-bars. Planes come in low over the water to land, metres above the heads of swimmers.

"Oh my god," Beyza says, "they fly so low. Is that safe?"

"Of course. They have people telling them what to do."

"No, I mean, like, the water. Don't planes run on kerosene and loads of other chemical stuff?"

"Well, yeah. But it doesn't come pouring out into the sea just because they're about to land," I laugh.

Beyza does, too. As we sit back against our sunbeds and watch another one fly in, however, I find myself fixating on its engine. I have never considered this before.

We wade into the sea, wincing as the first waves lap at our waistbands, and swim out until we see a plane turning at the end of the bay. Then, having scared ourselves, we splash back towards the shore so that we are never directly underneath one. We sit panting in the shallows, craning our necks until it has landed, safely. Then we swim out again. The water turns colder around our ankles and shoulders before another pair of lights appears.

"Go," Beyza cries.

I can hardly keep up for the water I am swallowing, gasping with the hilarity of it, again and again. Minutes pass, then an hour. Exhausted, we drag ourselves out and collapse onto our sunbeds. There is the popping open of a lid, the reapplying of sun cream to each other's backs and the smell of it like a holiday that has become my everyday life. I squint up at the underside of our parasol, disbelieving. I have done it, I think, I am here. With her.

"Okay, new game. What airline do we think that is?" she asks.

I look up to see another plane, just far enough away to be indiscriminate. "Erm. British Airways?"

"How very middle class of you," she smiles, grimly. "I'll say EasyJet."

We are both wrong.

Again. "Aeroflot?"

"Emirates."

This time it is Lufthansa.

"Here comes another one," Beyza says, drumming her fingers on her thigh in anticipation. "Wizz? I keep seeing that. Never heard of it before."

"Okay then. I'll take EasyJet."

"Qatar again," she cries, when a second red and white jet descends into sight. She lays back into the sun that has crept across her bed, defeated.

"Do you want some shade?" I ask, preparing to up and move myself over.

"That's okay, I'll tan for a bit. Thanks."

As she says this, she adjusts her bikini top. The fabric is textured, slightly, scalene. The black ink compass beneath it catches my eye.

"I like your swimsuit," I say, shyly, when Beyza catches me looking.

"I like yours," she replies, "on you."

I feel my face redden, though my sunbed is in full shade.

We are in a second taxi, pulling out of the car park when she says, quietly, "My grandparents used to live there."

I look out the window at the sign to which she is pointing. "Before?"

She nods. Her snub nose is silhouetted by the backs of the beach bars, all in a row. One on the end catches my eye and I twist to see it grow smaller, just as the courts saw it shrivelled to size eighteen months ago. A legal case had achieved some rare success, a displaced citizen wanting their land back; whoever had built on it, evidently, had not sought the permission of its owner on the Other Side. Now the building decays, and nothing new can be put in its place. Its white wood is grubby and rotting, ruining the look of the neighbouring businesses.

"Have they been back to their house? Since," I ask, stiffly.

Beyza's head is still turned so I can't see her face. "They tried," she says, to her window, "but the new occupants wouldn't let them in."

At this, I blink. *We're the same*. The glass reflects my girlfriend's words back at both of us. *Just the same*. She lets me take her hand, though she still won't turn to face me. I picture the compass on her ribcage stopping into sudden silence, and it makes my head spin.

Thirty-Six

"Nice neighbourhood," Beyza says.

I have invited her over the border again, this time to stay the night at my flat. The weight of this invitation swells with the heat in the air between us. I feel close to her, feel my eyes and lips turn bright and wide as hers do, involuntarily, when we look at each other.

It is past five o'clock when we reach my great grandfather's building. The sun has been sinking lower, and now the sky is a dusky pink. I draw my keys out jangling and the door pulls away from me.

"Maria," I start.

She appears more cloaked than ever by the frayed hood of her hair, too hot for this summer evening. I wonder why it looks so much darker, whether she has dyed it. Then I realise that I have not seen her since I spoke to my mother, about 'the incident'.

"Hallo," Maria coos, putting on her sunglasses.

She is on her way out. Still, she inclines her head towards Beyza, expectantly.

With a strained smile, I introduce my 'friend' as another girl who grew up in London while her family remained on this island. I do not specify which side of the island, and when Maria addresses Beyza in what she presumes is their shared native language, I say quickly, "Oh, no. Her parents only spoke English at home. She doesn't understand."

"I have to learn," Beyza says, apologetically.

She also stays quiet. About the second language that she does in fact speak, the language that everyone speaks on the Other Side.

"You will learn easily," Maria assures her, "now that you are here."

A kitten scurries up to her sandaled feet, then darts back between shrubs.

"Nice meeting you, anyway."

"Thanks. You too."

Still smiling, she carries on to her car. The smell of bubblegum lingers where she stood inside the door. I let it slam shut behind us and start up the darkened staircase.

"So that was your aunt?" Beyza asks, over my shoulder.

"Yeah."

"She seems nice."

"Yeah," I repeat, hollowly.

I feel sick after our encounter, knowing what I know now. My revulsion is disorientating, making me want to lash out at Beyza for her possessive need to establish that Maria was a relative, and not a threat, before saying that she seemed nice. Must everyone be vetted like this? I pick my pace up, up the three flights of stairs to my flat, leaving my girlfriend to trail after me, panting.

"Are you okay?" she asks, inside.

Another door shuts, gentler at her touch.

I shake my head and sink onto the sofa that was my grandparents', then my aunt's, and that now is mine. "I'm fine," I say.

For a moment, Beyza watches me, sceptically. Then she reaches into her rucksack and pulls out a rectangular pack. It is battered and sealed with a figure eight of elastic band.

"I brought the pictures you asked for."

I turn my face up to look at her. "The ones we talked about?"

"Yeah."

Stepping closer, Beyza passes me the envelope. Our conversation in the taxi comes to mind, her telling me about the things that her grandparents found when they first moved into their city home. Among them were these photographs, left behind by the family who had lived there before in their rush to escape the siege. The elastic band flecks off under my fingers, falling away from them. It has lost its stretch.

"And your grandparents have kept these, all this time?"

"Since the seventies, yeah."

"Wow."

Beyza leaves me to my unwrapping, reviewing. I can hear her zipping and unzipping the chequered pockets of her bag on the table behind me, but all I can think of is this family. Their faces reflect the light between my fingers and thumb. A couple. Two children who could be theirs, or could be one of them with a sibling in their youth. A family portrait. Are they the parents there? I think so. The age of the prints makes it hard to tell.

"Why?" I whisper. I raise my voice so that Beyza can hear me, but not my eyes, not from the last picture. "Why did your grandparents hold on to this stuff?"

Slowly, she comes around to stand before me. She has reapplied her red lipstick so that her mouth is a fine point amidst the curls of her mane.

"Because it's someone's. It's memories. Wherever that family went, this will mean something to them. My grandmother always thought they might come back for it one day. But," Beyza shrugs, "I guess not."

I drop her gaze. She leans over the headshot I am clutching, of a boy in army uniform with a moustache. I stare at it, certain that he was even younger when it was taken than the graininess admits. I keep staring until he has bleared.

"Are you sure you're okay?"

With a shake of my head, I slot the photographs back.

"What's wrong?"

"It's nothing. Sorry."

Beyza creeps closer. She sits down beside me and the sofa flags.

I exhale into my palms. "My family has been through some stuff lately. I just found out about it."

When I say nothing more, she replies, "Well, every family goes through stuff."

"Not like this," I say.

The young soldier peeks out, sternly, from a corner of the envelope. Upon seeing him, I bury my face in Beyza's neck and smell the hair that she has let loose again.

"Like what?"

I feel the vibration of her voice in my temple. It sounds level, and yet I get the sense that she is annoyed by my wanting to be comforted without talking about why. There is a stiffness in her shoulders, like she is refraining from snapping at me to come out with it, stop withholding from her, on every front. Even this sensitive one. With a sniff, I sit upright again. Her brown eyes are fixed upon me.

"My mom called the other day," I begin.

As I proceed to tell her what Deborah told me, Beyza's arm slackens around my shoulders; I am letting her in. Though I do so reluctantly at first, it makes me feel better to talk, to hear my thoughts and feelings echoed back at me by this person who is determined to see through my eyes. To see out of them, it seems. We could not be sitting any closer together.

"I'm sorry," Beyza says, when I have told her everything. How outwardly ambivalent my aunt was, how desperate Shehani and how vulnerable Rita. She holds me close. "It is so important to be looked after, for everyone."

I get up to turn on the fan with her words resounding in my head, resonating as strongly as a passion. When I sit back down, it is on her lap, to kiss her until that passion is alive between us. I want her now more than ever, her hands on my thighs and mine under her top, hers raking, mine fumbling with the clasp of her bra. It springs undone soundlessly, yet the breath startles from both our lungs. I rub up and down her bare back while she undoes my shorts.

"Should we go to your bedroom?"

"No." There is no time now. That time has passed here already, with Paris, and cannot be repeated.

Rolling off the sofa, I wind the shutters down and crawl back towards Beyza, willing her mood not to have been broken by the noise and disruption. She takes my head between her palms and leans hers back into the cushions as I push apart her knees, rise up on mine. A point of contact at the tip of my tongue, a gasp and I see everything: we are two sides of a city, two schools of thought on God, two girls. Just two girls. She pulls me back onto the sofa with her.

We spend the rest of the evening braless, walking around in oversized T-shirts and our underwear. There is something about seeing Beyza stroll barefoot across my floors that simultaneously soothes and intoxicates me. I cook pasta and apologise for the warm hang of vinegar in the kitchen; it keeps the ants at bay. We listen to the music on her phone while we eat, drink cheap red wine and laugh. All the while, I think about her statement: it is so important to be looked after. I do feel looked after now that the two of us are alone together. It is wonderful. But as soon as we leave our private sphere and other people are involved, people looking and talking, people for Beyza to get jealous about, I feel that I have to look *out*. For trouble.

"So what do you want to do with those pictures?" she asks, when we are smoking on the balcony, just drunk enough that the world looks like her red lipstick; smudged, slightly, outside the lines.

"I don't know," I reply, turning my cigarette around to see that I have only half lit it.

She tips her head back, oblivious. Lets a long breath out to dissipate amongst the stars. "Does it get better than this?"

"No, it doesn't," I say.

But it does get worse.

Thirty-Seven

'One more sleep!' says the text from my mother.

I look around my flat. It needs another clean before my parents see it. It needs, I fear, to be cleansed of Beyza's presence, which has remained in the air since she stayed over last week. Beyza who I had hoped that text was from. We have been messaging back and forth since that night, the constant chime of my phone drowning out the noise of any niggling doubts in my head. Odd shoes on the floor. A forgotten coffee mug. A smear like warm breath on the balcony door, where she slid it open by its glass.

Could you tell, if you didn't know, what had happened in this room, recently and between two women? One of them being me and the other, *truly* other, being from the Other Side. Maria's painting draws my eye, and I tell myself that it is only me who sees Beyza in it; another person might see any two girls. Maria and I. Maria and Lim. Shehani and Atay.

I drop my thumbnail from my teeth. Perhaps not any two girls. The latter pair, certainly, would not huddle so close together. I have never seen Shehani as desperate to get away from her co-worker as she has seemed in the last few days. It must be difficult to live and work in such close quarters, I think, especially if you are uncomfortable with someone. I look away from the painting. Perhaps she would be glad to help me up here again, after my shift. To get away.

The air is hot but mercifully dry when I leave the building. The only hint of moisture is trickling from a watering can as I come around to Rita's veranda, which makes me smile. I step in through the gate, and stop. It creaks shut behind me. Atay is watering the bougainvillaea. But this is one of Shehani's jobs. Every day, I see her do it. I am unable to stop my brow from furrowing, following the spout of the can down into the dirt. Where is she?

My grandmother shocks me from my stupor.

"Today is the last day," she cries, her dark eyes keen and her hair less kempt than ever, "and then your parents will be with us." She throws her arms over my shoulders.

"Not long now," I say, hugging her back. Tomorrow, one less family member will be missing from her life. "Is Shehani around?"

Eliza steps away from me. "Shehani is sick. She is spending this morning in bed and we will see how she feels later. Why?" she asks, her taciturnity shifting towards alarm. "Do you need something?"

"Oh. No. I was just going to ask if she could help me upstairs, but that doesn't matter. Is she okay?"

"Well," Eliza says, ignoring my question, "if I stay with Rita for a bit this afternoon, you can take Atay up to help you. I don't mind."

The sound of running water stops. I look up to find that Atay is staring at me. The bottom falls out of my stomach. She turns and goes inside.

"Erm," I say, my mouth dry, "yeah. Maybe. I'll see what time I get back from work. I might be able to handle it myself, anyway."

"You let us know," Eliza says, pleasantly.

An engine starts in the garage and I make my excuses to leave.

"Hallo," Maria says, as I shut myself in the car beside her.

The tension in my shoulders does not ease. I can smell my grandmother's perfume from the squeeze she gave them, and smoke from the cigarette that my aunt must just have smoked. This is the first time we have carpooled since I found out about the incident, since I noticed the dispassion of my family's referrals to Rita's carers, even if one of them saved her life.

Maria tries and fails to start at least three conversations with me.

At last, I say, "Shehani is sick."

"Ah, yes. She hasn't been feeling well for a while, I think," Maria replies, airily.

Yet she turns the radio on to some glaringly upbeat music, and does not try to engage me again.

I am halfway through another shift at Chest, sweating through my T-shirt. I am grumbling at every customer, making eye contact only when they want something selfish and instantly gratifying from me; they are consumers, literally, consum*ing* and not caring about anything bigger, and I am sick of it. Then the door swings open. I stop still with two iced coffees in my hands.

"Daniela . . ."

"One with soya milk?"

"Yes please."

"And one regular," I say, bending to place the drinks down in front of an older couple. "Enjoy." I smile too broadly, then stride too purposefully back towards the till.

"Daniela," the voice sounds again, over my shoulder. It is at once restrained and commanding, and still I do not turn. I slide a tray out from under the back bar. My path back into the room is blocked.

"Hey."

"Get out of my way please, Paris."

His topknot shakes in time with his head.

"I have a job to do."

With a short breath out through his nose, Paris steps aside.

"Thank you."

I don't let myself meet his eye, or look at the scar above it, though it is winking at me. He has won me over with cocksure charm at every turn. Except the last one.

247

Paris follows me to a recently vacated table, and I begin loading glasses onto my tray.

"Can I talk while you work, at least?"

There is a clatter as I pile one cake plate onto another. The crumbs wobble.

"I made a mistake bringing that other girl here. I didn't know this was where you worked."

I snort.

"But I shouldn't have done it anyway, I get that. I'm not used to being messed around or made to wait for a text back, I guess. The mind games. That put me off."

"Mind games?" I repeat, tossing the last napkin onto my tray. It doesn't land with the impact I need it to, and I simmer, "It put you off when I kept you waiting *once*, but you had no problem doing it to me all the time?"

For the first time, I look directly at him, his eyebrows raised, his lips pursed. I think compulsively of our night together and then have to look away again, lift my tray, defiantly, to my chest. The sight of his stubble and all his straight edges still makes me blush. But I am able to separate passing pleasure from actual fulfilment now, I am struck to realise, to separate one whim from what I actually want, long term. Chris wanders out of the kitchen and I lower my voice. Calm.

"I don't want to see you again, so. If that's why you're here . . ."

Paris stares at me. "Is there someone else?" he asks, as if this can be the only reason.

"No," I say. "This isn't about anyone else."

And I mean it. With or without Beyza, I would not take Paris back. I am getting closer to some kind of understanding, knowing what I do *not* want. I am crossing things off, one at a time. First, him.

I carry the dirty plates into the kitchen and come back out with a cloth in my hand, bend to wipe down the table. As I watch Paris leave, my eyes linger on the door swinging shut behind him, and I wish it would slam, once and for all, behind me.

Thirty-Eight

Midmorning. I have the day off, and so far have spent it finishing what I started last night: cleaning my flat. Alone, in the end, since Shehani was still in bed sick and I didn't want to invite Atay upstairs. The thought unnerved me, for reasons I could not explain. I shake it from my head, lock my front door shut behind me. My parents are due any moment now. We have planned to meet them at Rita's for a welcome coffee, but as I walk down and around to my great aunt's flat, it is Shehani that I think of. I don't remember her getting sick like this, ever, and I hope harder with every step that she has woken up feeling better.

She hasn't, as it turns out.

"Good morning, my love."

"Hallo, hallo. How are you?"

I know as soon as I walk in—to hugs from my grandparents and a smile from George—that there is a sick person here. Not Rita, who fixes me with unseeing eyes, head rolled back against her armchair at a rag doll's angle. Rita has been in this state for a long time, and her flat has not been filled so inescapably with this stale air of death. There is someone else, I sense, suffering something different. More acute.

"Is Shehani still unwell? Can I see her?"

"You must let her rest," Eliza says, lowering her eyelids with what could be exasperation or sympathy.

There is a muffled cough from down the corridor, behind a closed bedroom door, and I stare desperately after the sound. Then there is another, outside: an engine shuddering into silence.

"They're here," my grandmother breathes.

Only Andreas beats her to the veranda. She, George and I follow him out, just in time to see my father lifting a suitcase from Maria's boot. He is straining under the weight of the many books inside, Andreas insisting upon opening and closing the passenger door for my mother. When she thanks him, he bows and says 'not at all' with exaggerated courteousness. They both laugh. Then my parents are on the veranda and more greetings, more hugs, more smiles are being exchanged.

"We have missed you," my grandmother is crooning, draping herself over Deborah's shoulder, as if either one of them could stand to spend more than five minutes with the other.

"We've missed you too," my mother says.

She smooths her skirt when they pull apart, a knee-length A-line garment that I think she could wear to work in a diner, if it were yellow instead of white. I bow my head as she approaches.

"Hi, honey." She stops. Too close to me, as always.

I inhale shallowly, self-conscious of my breath for the first time since I left England, where the people around me ate politely and my mother was never far off blowing up or melting

251

down. Whatever it was, spittle or tears, always wet me at this proximity.

"Hi."

She steps even closer. In her arms, I smell sleep-must and ethanol from all the hand sanitizer she will have applied on the plane. I remember her buffing it into the tray tables on others, like Dettol. Then her palms are on my shoulders, pressing me backwards, pinning me there, her blue eyes intent on mine.

"You look well," she says, at last.

She stretches to a smile and I sag with relief.

"Dani . . ."

My father's beard looks even bushier than it did when I left London, which Eliza bristles at, ever afraid for him. I cherish the scratchy feel of it on my neck when he pulls me close.

"Let us sit down," my great grandfather chitters.

And we all troop inside, my parents taking turns to bend before Rita and let her clutch their fingers like a baby, wide-eyed, as they say slow hallos to her. Jason appears to be holding back tears, which makes me want to be near him. We sit side by side on the sofa.

"Atay," Eliza calls, twice.

A door opens and closes. I taste dust from the many bookshelves and, after a moment, Atay appears.

"Ah, here you are. Can we have some coffee, please? Nescafes for our two girls," Eliza says, grouping my aunt with me again as un-adult, unaccountable. "And Deborah? My Jason?"

Everyone gets their orders in and with a nod, Atay withdraws. The tap is run, the fans drone on. And yet the room feels quiet.

My father lowers his voice, accordingly. "So this is the new girl?"

"Yes," Eliza says at her usual volume, "Atay."

"And where is Shehani?" my mother asks.

As if on cue, Shehani coughs again, and Eliza explains with a tight smile that she is in bed sick.

"Oh gosh," my mother chuckles, "I can't imagine being sick now, in this heat."

While everyone laughs in agreement—Deborah has never fared well here in high summertime—she fans herself with her hand, basking in the attention.

"It is very hot," George says, turning solemn. His moustache stills before he adds, "Thirty-six degrees already this morning. Early."

"Thirty-six?" Maria tuts. "I was thinking of going to swim, but . . ."

The smell of coffee precedes Atay's return to the room. She sets the tray down, then sets herself down in Shehani's place beside Rita. As my family carry on through her spluttering, complacent, the skin of my forehead feels tighter.

"Wow. She could cough a little louder, couldn't she?" my father says, in English.

All our talk now is in English, all for my mother's benefit. She chuckles as her in-laws did at her joke, moments ago, shaking their heads. Only now, Atay joins them, emitting a laugh that splays at its top note with glee. I gape at her. This is the first time I have heard her make a sound, or seen any expression on her face but a dark stare. Her teeth are sharp, her tongue a spear of pink. She looks human, even juvenile, and yet the bones dissolve from my legs.

"Do you think it's safe for her to be near Rita like this?"

"Well. Soon enough . . ."

To a grave nod from my father, my grandmother spreads her hands; they must have talked about my great aunt's impending move into a hospice already.

There is silence.

"I like your necklace, Dani," my mother says.

My fingers find the ovals at my collarbones. Copper. The element that unites us, I think, distractedly. It feels cold.

Shehani's coughing becomes violent. There is a thump like her falling out of bed or pounding the wall, she is gasping for air and our eyes are widening, my father running into her room. Eliza and I follow close behind him. Shehani is on her knees, clutching her chest and trembling violently. There is a dark patch on her mattress and the smell of urine pervades, making me cover my mouth and nose in instinctive horror. At a cry from Eliza, Shehani looks up, her pupils constricted to pinpricks. One of us gasps.

"Get the phone, Daniela," Eliza says. "Get an ambulance."

The light goes completely out of Shehani's eyes. Jason drops to catch her and my grandmother pushes me back down the corridor.

"Dani," my mother starts, her voice sharp with warning.

I am unable to speak as I pick up the phone, wired to the wall where it was left to hang the last time someone needed a doctor; I can see the marks that they have yet to paint over. It won't happen again. Not like that, I think, I am here to make sure.

"*Dani.*"

"She needs an ambulance," I say.

There is an intake of breath across the room. I lock eyes with my aunt. Hers grow large before settling into an acceptance that might be relief; this time, everyone is going to be okay, and the call is not hers to make.

Beyond

Thirty-Nine

I called in sick to work this morning. I feel sick, truthfully enough, after what happened to Shehani, what has been happening to Shehani over the course of weeks and months, slowly. A dose at a time, Atay has been poisoning her. This is what my grandmother tells me as we drive to the hospital, in a tone like she is pinching some foul-smelling thing between the tips of her fingers. Eyes watering, mouth downturned.

"Are you sure you want to go?" my mother asked me, earlier.

"Yes," I said, "I want to make sure Shehani is okay. I want to see her."

Eliza urged my parents to go ahead with their plans to see friends, eat lunch somewhere nice, perhaps go to the sea. This was still their holiday after all. "I will take Daniela to the hospital. I'm going anyway," she said.

I feel far from her, though I am only in the passenger seat. Radio hosts blather between us, louder and louder until they fall apart laughing and Eliza punches them into silence. The air conditioning whistles through the vents like gritted teeth.

"You know, Shehani has been trying to warn me about Atay for some time," she says.

At this, my eyes widen. I try not to let them stray beyond the power button, still singing with her assault.

259

"The first thing she told me was that sometimes, in the middle of the night, she would wake up to see Atay standing over her, just staring. I told her she must be dreaming."

I nod, remembering this conversation. It took place on Rita's veranda; I overheard it from inside the bathroom and came out to find that Atay, too, had been listening. I think of her finger held to her lips like a candle in some illicit night, and then of Shehani's tears nights later, her bare feet pounding the pavement as she fled the flat. Perhaps Atay had been watching her then.

"Well. Some weeks ago, she started complaining about her shampoo. She said it was irritating her scalp, but she always used the same brand and had never had a problem before."

"I remember her scratching," I say, as my grandmother switches lanes and the ground shifts sideways beneath us.

"Yes," Eliza affirms, "she told me that you said she should try a different product, and I agreed. So she did."

Breaking ahead of a right-turn, she flicks her indicator on. It ticks, ticks, ticks.

"But she had the same problem. Every shampoo she used made her itch, and as time went on, it got so bad—the last one was burning her, she told me—she scratched until she bled."

I close my eyes as we round the corner, tasting bile. "Why would Atay do this?"

My grandmother sighs. "Sometimes, not a lot, but occasionally, they do. You hear stories. I mean, they are desperate, these people. We bring them from very poor countries to look after our loved ones, but they have loved ones of their own to look after. You can't forget that. We don't know what their situation is. We see their CV online, maybe we talk to them once and if they seem clean, professional, then we sponsor their work visa. It's not easy to know if they are good until they are here." Hands on the wheel, Eliza shrugs her shoulders. "It's the risk we take."

"But this is more than not being *good*," I say, aghast.

"It is, yes. Well. Maybe Atay has some friend or relative she wants to bring here, and they need the visa. So if she succeeded to scare Shehani away, maybe she would recommend this other person to replace her. We don't know."

"Does that happen?" I ask.

"Unfortunately, in some rare cases, it does."

"That's extreme."

"It is extreme," my grandmother says, making a final turn into the hospital car park. Up and down the grey and white grid, she drives, searching for a space. No one has parked neatly inside the lines. "And sometimes they lie, also. Or they make a mistake. That's why I wasn't sure when Shehani told me, at first. And now this." At last, she turns off the engine, bows her head and lets her

261

hands hit the steering wheel with tears in her eyes. "I should have listened. I should have believed her."

"You didn't know," I try to comfort her.

"But I am listening now. I took her shampoo to a lab to be tested for poison, so we will see if it was that. Or maybe Atay gave it to her some other way. I don't know." Eliza sniffs.

"You will," I promise her, "soon."

I am filled with an iron will to help in any way that I can, remembering Beyza's statement once again: it is so important to be looked after, for everyone. Taking a deep breath, I get out of the car with my grandmother and we go inside to see Shehani.

"How is she?" my mother asks, in a low voice.

An ant reaches the top of the table leg. I say nothing and she doesn't notice. It is just the two of us sitting out on Rita's veranda. Everyone else is inside, minding her, minding Atay. No one has said anything about the lab testing for poison. We don't want to raise Atay's suspicions before the results come back—she cannot be arrested or deported until then—nor can we leave her with Rita, unsupervised, in the meantime.

"Shehani is in a bad way," I murmur, thinking of the coloured wires like veins outside her body in the hospital bed. Thinking of Atay standing over it, or just inside the front door. I shake myself.

"But they say she will recover. We got her to the hospital just in time."

"Good," my mother muses. She lets her hand fall from her chin to the table, then sees the ant and retracts it. "Do you believe that Atay did this?"

"Yes," I say, louder in my surprise. "Don't you?"

Deborah's elbows are still in the air. She doesn't look up from the insect to say, "I believe there's more to every story than meets the eye."

A warm wind blows. Behind her, the bougainvillaea that Shehani tended to sways from side to side, and I shake my head along with its stems. I cannot imagine that smiling, sensitive woman, who has been in my life long enough to see her daughter grow from toddler to teenager to adult, all through me, being anything but the victim in this. Atay meanwhile, ever silent . . .

My mother scoffs. The ant appears to have found something of interest and keeps crawling in circles in front of her, until she moves to the opposite end of the table.

I catch myself in a sneer. Atay is *so* silent, I realise, that I have no idea whether she is also a mother, a caring daughter or a wife, no idea of the ties that might be pulling her in any particular direction. Perhaps her heart aches beneath that cold exterior. Perhaps she has been working to feed fifteen people in the Philippines, or perhaps she is the loneliest woman in the world. What do I know?

"I know she did this," I repeat, with less conviction.

I remember my grandmother's words, *sometimes they lie*, and I wonder whether Shehani might have as desperate a reason to want Atay out as Atay might have her. It is impossible to say, and unfair to condemn Atay just because of her quietude, when Shehani could easily be hiding something behind her beaming and her baking. I don't want to believe this after so many years, but I see now; I cannot discount it. Shehani has a daughter.

"It's one woman's word against another's. That never ends well," my mother sighs, adjusting herself in her seat. "Anyway. Eliza says she's going to start looking into hospices. It's time to move Rita somewhere safer, more stable. So there'll be no more of this."

I look again at the ant going round and round after something I cannot see, not a crumb, not a smear that it can lap up or carry away with it. And yet it persists. It grows smaller as I sit back, understanding; Shehani might indeed have been desperate enough to corrupt her own shampoo. For months, Eliza has talked about keeping just one worker here without Rita, to clean and to wait for her father's decay; she will be prepared for that as she was not for her mother's.

Suddenly the racket of crickets is deafening. I wish there was something I could do to help, to make it so these women's situations were not so dire that they fled their own homes and became territorial over other people's, possessive of jobs like scrubbing the toilets inside and helping old people use them, because if their co-workers proved too useful they risked being sent back again. They cannot afford to see their children. They work twenty-four hours, live-in, get one day off a week and are grateful. It is no life.

I open my mouth to express this, but all that comes out is, "I'm not happy, Mom."

Deborah nods as if she knows this already. The blonde hair that makes her so exotic here is browning in the afternoon sun, like something taken off the heat just in time. "We're very proud of you for coming here by yourself, you know, your father and I. You've settled in so well," she says.

Her praise touches me, gently, on the back of my shoulder. With my mind's eye, I turn to see what has escaped my notice, what she casts her passing shine on like a lighthouse might a rock.

"I know I have. I just feel like there's so much more that I could be doing. Should be doing," I whisper, afraid of *myself* overhearing me now, the self that clamoured for years to get out of England. This move was supposed to answer my questions and make me content, not more restless even than I was before.

"Like what?" my mother asks, leaning towards me. "What is it that would make you happy, Dani? Because whatever it is, you shouldn't waste time *feeling* like doing it. You should just do it. Otherwise . . ."

In demonstration, she waves a hand in the direction of Rita's flat. The place where Rita has remained stationary for fifteen years, waiting to die and rejoin her late husband. The place where Shehani was poisoned in a desperate effort either her own or her colleague's. The place where I have had coffee with my family most days before setting out to discover more of myself in the hot sun. At last, I have come to a conclusion.

"I have to make a phone call," I say.

Forty

It is evening when I arrive at the border, in thin-soled sandals that the dust turns stippled and grubby beneath my feet. I shift from one to the other in the line behind two men in business suits, look over my shoulder. There is no one behind me. Invisible cars swish past under the lilac sky, tinged with the sun's last yellow over one side of the city. My side of the city; it has set on Beyza's.

"Yes please."

I face forwards. A UN officer is leaning out of his booth, his bald head tipped towards me, the face upon it small and stern.

"I just need to get in there," I explain, pointing to a building beyond his ribbed metal office as the men before me did.

Music pulses from inside. Laughter sounds. It is a bar, I have been told, the only one allowed to function inside the city's buffer zone.

With a tacit nod, the UN officer waves me through. "Just make sure you come out the right way," he says, with a grim smile.

Mine fades as I take a few steps past him, towards the armed men waiting in an identical booth on the Other Side. Aside from the music, I cannot believe how quiet it is here, given how central. To my right, beyond the bar restored from crumbling, there are wrought iron railings. The city falls away into a park beneath the square. Then there is a quarter renowned for its beautiful architecture, leftover from another occupation. Lights glow in the windows of those houses that have not been shuttered into darkness for the night, but I cannot see the rooms inside. They are on the Other Side.

On my left, overshadowing all this, is a site that I think might be the most stunning of all: the hotel. It is made of the same golden brick that everything I admire is, with white pillars upholding the pointed arches of its entrance and matchbox balconies for every room. Its great doors were flung open, once, to artists and the elite, for balls and cocktail parties. Gazing upwards, I can hear strings as though they are still being plucked inside, until footsteps sound and I am back in the present, backed by an automated beat. I blink up at the white trimming around the flat roof like the edge of a birthday cake, all flourish and no flavour now, with the barbed wire in front of it. Bullet holes tarnish the walls. This is where the UN have their headquarters, where they oversee occasional meetings between the leaders of our divided island, and nothing changes.

"Hey." The footsteps stop.

I turn to see Beyza hovering across the border like a mirage, in clean trainers and red lipstick to match her T-shirt dress. Its hems hang long over her elbows and knees so that she appears jointless, smoothly finished right up to her hijab. White, this evening.

"Hi." I put my arms around her, smell smoke and that talcum powder. What does she use it for?

"How are you?"

"Good. It's good to see you."

"Yeah, I missed you. You look nice."

"You too," I say, my throat hoarse.

Drawing back, I see that the fabric of her hijab is stretched thin over her hair; there are bumps where she has bound down its waves, and in the bold liner on her eyelids.

"Have I seen this before?" she asks, lifting a corner of my skirt.

A breeze blows around my legs and I shiver, despite its warmth. "Maybe not. I haven't worn it much."

"It's cute on you."

"Thanks." I look at the fold between her finger and thumb, blue piqued with white flowers, and smile.

"Shall we go inside?"

"Actually, there's something I thought we could do first."

She frowns at the pack I produce, sealed with a new elastic band.

"The photos?"

269

"I did some research. Apparently there are ways of finding these people. We could track down the family, restore some of their history. Their memories."

"Now that there's the technology," we say at once.

"And social media," Beyza adds.

"I'm sure that's part of it, yeah. It's, like, a facial recognition thing."

"It must be," she agrees. "But how would we do it? I didn't think just anyone could use those programs. That would be dodgy, wouldn't it?"

I laugh. "Yeah, maybe not. But I have another idea."

We approach the guarded hotel gates.

"Excuse me," I say, to one of several officers inside, "we have some photographs."

"My grandparents found them after the conflict," Beyza says, leaning in. "They were left in their house . . ."

An officer puts his hand through the bars between us, a neutral force. He takes the envelope, unwinds its band and fans one or two pictures out in front of him. A colleague peers over his shoulder, silent, then moves on. Like he has seen this before. Like it has happened a lot in the years since the invasion, since displacement and the misplacement of all anyone ever owned has become normal, and nothing has been done about it. Except perhaps this can be done about it. Perhaps uniting people with pictures can provide some small recompense for their losses, for the Elizas of this island—both sides of it—who lost their mothers too young. Let me tell you about where I live, I want to burst forth and tell the world. There were photographs left swinging on the walls of homes, yes, but those who came in afterwards *did* care. My great grandmother was not one of a thousand who went missing amidst the unrest, but one of *two* thousand; the Other Side lost, too. I know this now.

"Thank you." The UN officer withdraws with our envelope.

"Was that it?" Beyza asks.

"I guess, yeah."

"Wow. That was easy."

I study the fold of her brow, the uneven slope of her nose and one twisted corner of her mouth, until she looks back at me.

"*Now* can we get a drink?"

"Okay," I relent.

But I walk as slowly towards the bar as she will allow me.

We end up sitting outside at a table overlooking the park. Palms and pines sway both above and below us, while the sun sinks lower and the sky turns to violet. The music is loud, but not too lairy. A table away, I see the businessmen who came in before me sitting with two others—*Other* others—a layer of paperwork spread over their white tablecloth. They must work for a bi-communal business. We are in the one venue in the city where meetings like this are possible, I suppose. How many of the groups around us are here for the same reason?

"So, I didn't feel right doing this on my side," I mumble, fiddling with the stem of my cocktail glass, "or yours. I thought we should meet in the middle."

Beyza stops mid-sip to stare at me. Her glass is short and square, much stabler looking than mine. It contains something rum-based, I think, and is full of crushed ice.

"Does this have anything to do with that *thing* you wanted to talk about?"

I nod.

She takes another drink, puts her glass down and stares harder.

I breathe out. "I can't carry on like this with you. It's nothing to do with our history. Or any history," I add, gesturing at the hotel, which now looks looming in the twilight, "but I'm leaving. One of us was always going to. I guess we both just thought it would be you. At the end of the summer," I clarify, when Beyza maintains her silence.

Laughter explodes at another table.

"Please say something."

She sits back. Reaches into her pocket, pulls out a cigarette. "You know, I was actually thinking about staying. Trying to get a job here, like you. *For* you," she says, with one corner of her mouth. There is the flash of her lighter before she scoffs, "I should have known better."

"No," I say, with tears welling, "you shouldn't have. Things have been good with us. Really good," I persist, "I've loved all our time together. But there's some stuff I need to do, and I can't do it here. Or in England. Not like I want to."

Beyza drags an ashtray towards her, tarnished. "What stuff?" she asks.

She still looks stung, but there is a curiousness to her eyes now, a crack of openness to explanation that makes me hope, wholeheartedly, she will understand.

Forty-One

"Ladies and gentlemen," an announcement begins, with a sound like the seatbelt sign.

My grandmother searches the warehouse-high ceiling as though to catch sight of the man making it. Is she holding back tears? It is hard to tell with the strip lights reflecting off her pupils. She was emotional this morning, following her pats of my shoulder with extra squeezes, reminding me that my family would always be here for me.

"Wherever you are, whatever you need," she said.

She kept nodding, profusely, until I thanked her for the fifth time.

She cups my shoulder again, which prompts Andreas to hand over my rucksack.

"It is time," my great grandfather says. He laughs in his chirruping way, moustache twitching. But there is weariness in his eyes.

Maria tucks her hand into the crook of his elbow. She looks as lost as he does amidst the white floor, the white walls, the criss-cross of coloured signs for 'arrivals' and 'departures' and 'toilets' and 'taxis', the swathes of people bundling into each other after different destinations. Children shout, couples squabble. Another chime sounds overhead and we all look up, instinctively. Why

274

George and my aunt chose to drive to the airport in convoy with us, I don't know. Now that I have dropped off my suitcase, there is nothing to do but say goodbye. I suppose they wanted every last moment. Do they suppose these *are* our last moments?

"Ah, my love. We will miss you," Eliza says, her scribbled brows drawing together.

"I'll be back," I assure her, stepping in for a hug.

She squeezes me tight and thumps my back, hard. Her eyes are definitely shinier. Perhaps she will cry after all.

"This is home now," I say, never mind the one-way ticket weighing heavy in my hand.

"Oh." My grandfather draws out this syllable, head cocked, palms raised. "So, shall we take you back with us now?"

I laugh and hug him, too. Then my aunt, whose static hair tickles the inside of my ear.

"Are you wearing a bikini?" I ask her, pulling back.

The aqua-blue strap over her shoulder has caught my eye.

"Yes," she admits, giggling. "The sea is there, so I thought if George drives back with my parents, maybe I'll go . . ." Sheepishness shades her face.

"Why not?" I smile, turning back to my great grandfather. "You have to make the most of it, don't you? It's going to start getting cooler soon."

"Thirty-five today," he announces, with a wag of his index finger. "It is still too much."

"Yes. But . . ." I hold my arms around him, eyes closed. "It won't be long now. Thank you all, for everything."

They watch me check in with sad eyes and strong smiles, and wave until I have turned the corner out of their sight. Loading my rucksack onto a conveyor belt, I wait to be summoned through a metal-detecting doorframe, tongue pressed to the roof of my mouth. Fingers flex. I step towards them through the green-lit passage, holding my breath until I see that it has not turned red. Security has not seen through me, newly jobless and single.

Well, no. I swing my rucksack onto my back. Not jobless. I have resigned from my role as Front of House Assistant, yes, but I am on my way to start something new, somewhere I have never been before. I have kept in contact with my parents since their return to England some weeks ago, kept them up to date with my research and applications until at last, someone came back to me. A woman. Her voice was at once apologetic and urgent over the phone; she sounded sceptical yet excited about me coming to work for her organisation, in a rare paid position.

"Those are like gold dust in the charity world," my mother commended me.

"They are," my father echoed. He must have been close enough to kiss her.

"Well done."

She sounded happy, though she was concerned for my safety. Everyone was.

It didn't matter. For the first time in my life, I didn't second guess my decision. I was determined to go and do good in a place where bad things had been done, exclusively, for years and years. And so I am going. There are troubles in this city, in this country, it is true, but they are at a stalemate and I want to act. The rest of the world refers to this as our problem, officially. Meanwhile, our leaders talk big and do little. Nothing moves. Not freely; people need passports to get to their old homes, to their offices, to those they might love most in the world. Some protest. Several are violent. But there is rarely enough blood spilled at once to generate a response, a resolution. Not that there should have to be.

I think of my aunt's Sister Hanuni, whose assignments made her feel 'needed'. 'Treasured', Saxon said. Perhaps I didn't appreciate those motivations at the time, but theirs is a supportive community. From place to place across the world, they have built it. What is there for me to do here but spit and speculate, listen to the accusations of two women, no witnesses and an inconclusive poison test, until one of them is deported? Sit and fret. Keep sitting. Was it the right woman? We will never know. All the injustices have eaten away at me inside my family-owned flat, which I have never paid rent for. I couldn't understand or appeal to women like Shehani or Atay from so many storeys above them, not enough to make a difference.

When I reach my gate, I sit down and watch the planes beyond the window like a cinema screen, the clear sky and the sea beyond them. I think of my aunt stripping off to her swimsuit, how Beyza and I did the same along the bay, just out of sight.

I text her: 'I love you. I'm sorry. Thank you x'. Then I switch off my phone.

A plane turns onto the runway. Blue Air. I wonder if I would have got that from the beach. There sounds the faintest rumble through the glass and then it is off, accelerating from the ground with its back tilted up to the sun. When I can no longer see it, I lean back in my metal seat, unforgiving and cold from the air conditioning. I doubt there will be much of that where I am going, no matter how hot it gets. Going, but always coming back, I think. Hopefully to make a difference.

I am from this island and I am from another. I am of a woman who comes from a collection of states like different countries that make up a continent. I have the capacity to love both boys and girls, so much that I might settle down one day with one or the other, neither or both. I don't know yet but that is okay, I can choose to look at it as exciting because some uncertainty can be after all. And I am sure enough of other things, like what I want to do next. What I need to do. I should have felt it starting inside me behind the till in Oxfam, in bed with Beyza, in the one-room museum overlooking this stunning, severed city with Paris, and in so many other places. I need to help. I need to make whole things that are not, because the only truly certain thing is that the world is uncertain. Life is uncertain, constantly changing, and perhaps there is some reassurance in taking it as it comes. In its entirety, undivided. I want to go where there are no borders, no piled bricks, barbed wire fences or blood grudges going back decades. I want myself, my island and all the people upon it to be surrounded, as they should be, by love and only water. No more guarded crossing points, no more no-go zones. Here, in this city of halves, *I* have become whole. And now a new purpose: I will help others to be, everywhere.

Afterword

While I relied on the accounts of family members and friends for much of the detail in this novel, I also carried out extensive research. For me, there is no better way to inhabit a character than to method write them, and so I found myself exploring parts of Cyprus that I never had before, as well as attending a variety of religious services.

During this process, I spent time with a community of Jehovah's Witnesses, who were very welcoming. I would like to make clear that while several of their views caused the protagonist of this book to feel conflicted, my intention was not to portray their faith in a negative light. Every line of dialogue in the Watchtower Study scene was inspired, either by jw.org or by a service that I attended, and not imbued with my personal beliefs.

Likewise, Daniella's initial negative feelings towards 'The North' are not reflective of my own. In order to fully address the political situation in Cyprus, I felt it was important to acknowledge the reluctance to make amends which, sadly, a portion of the population feels. That being said, I know several people who, like Dani, have become more open-minded through a shared love of something. I hope to meet many more in the years to come.

Any factual errors in this text are mine alone.

Acknowledgements

To all those who have read this book from start to finish, I am indebted. If you're happy to share your thoughts, I'd love to read a review.

To hear more about upcoming releases, join my mailing list at https://eva-asprakis.mailchimpsites.com. You can also follow https://www.instagram.com/eva.asprakis/ on Instagram for glimpses of life in Cyprus, book recommendations and writing updates. Let's keep in touch.

To the friends whose calls I failed to return whilst writing this, thanks for your patience. I am sure I don't deserve it.

To my parents, thanks for your support, and for the years you spent reading to me.

To my wider family, thanks for your stories. I hope I have done them justice.

To Mark, thanks for the nudge, and for the 'palatably delivered' wisdom.

And Max, for your faith, I cannot thank you enough. You never cease to believe in me, even when I do. For that reason, this book, though I know you'll deny it, is as much a feat of your hard work as it is mine.

Thanks also to those few authors who became international bestsellers with their books set in Cyprus, who proved that people do, in fact, want to read about this wonderful island, and thus inspired me to keep writing.

Printed in Poland
by Amazon Fulfillment
Poland Sp. z o.o., Wrocław

13539965R00169